IN LIEU *of* EATING

IN LIEU *of* EATING

Jami Amerine

Copyright © 2023 Jami Amerine.

ISBN: 979-8-9866660-7-5

To Mom and Dad:

**In lieu of moving out of your house,
I wrote another book. I love you each and both.**

Life is the flower for which love is the honey.

—**Victor Hugo**

Aperitif

There is a natural order we human beings are accustomed to. Our stories begin with "Once upon a time." And are brought to a close with "The End." I, Clara Louise Honeycutt, love order. But I do not tell stories with words. Well, I mean, I am telling one now that way. But only to bring order to the stories that I tell with food.

That said:

Once upon a time, I owned a restaurant in Midtown Manhattan called Honey's, which would not be serving anything expected, yet would involve everything I could concoct to bring my culinary stories to life. Granted, "Authentic Southern Cooking" fused with "French Homestyle Cuisine" may have alarmed, and even possibly confused, critics. Until one of my "stories" rocketed me from Cinderella to the top of the food chain and then right back down again.

In the natural order of good food and great stories, I would suggest that the top is what we crave. Is that position not the evolution of all things? To not only strive but thrive? Again, order. Starters are the hook; the main course is the arc. And the joyful resolution is, of course, dessert. The coup de grace of any good meal is not found in the singular analysis of courses, flavors, textures, or aromas. It is the experience of the journey. From beginning to end, a perfect meal is an exploration of sensual cognition. And it is magnified in the ambiance of grand company. Hospitality is the only mark of heredity I hold in common with my exquisite mother. But I am not one of those *sugary-sweet, how can I bow to meet your expectations?* or *Please tell me you love me!* kind of beings. Which I deem both iconic and ironic because I go by the nickname *Honey*. Which is sweeter than me.

Honey, in its rawest form, fascinates and delights me. I love bees, though I am highly allergic to them. In culinary school, I wrote a paper clarifying the stabilization of honey's flavor at various temperatures. That "exposé" earned me an opportunity to write a weekly column for *The Fork*, a food and dining magazine subscribed to by over one million worldwide readers. The gig allowed me to work from my Upper Westside flat while simultaneously granting me the freedom to experiment with ingredients and perfect my craft.

I should also mention, my parents, Tom and Sylvie Honeycutt, live downstairs. They own the brownstone, of which I sometimes pay the rent on for the top-floor flat. Call it rent control. But I am no dummy. If not for my parents, I would have to work at least three jobs to live in New York on my own. My dad, a retired accountant with a mind that could thumb-wrestle Albert Einstein and win, is entirely brilliant and *hilarious*—that being the only reasonable explanation I can think of for how he was able to romance my mother, the legendary Sylvie Roman. A concert violinist for thirty-seven years, Sylvie, the world-renowned French melodic wonder, stands six inches taller than my father and speaks fluent Portuguese, French, Spanish, and, for some reason, Mandarin. Dad hails from Sawmill, Texas, where the town motto is "Big Heart, Small Town," and the employment rate is below 5 percent. To hear my dad tell the story, one would think he hadn't known that shoes existed until he was in college. The one-room schoolhouse where Dad "learnt stuff" had only one word that required spelling mastery for credit: Poverty.

While I suspect that tale was a lie or, at best, a wild exaggeration, Dad's college records weren't. Not only was my father the first of his family to graduate with a college degree, but he was also the only surviving member of his high school graduating class. Propane explosion—it really is too gruesome to discuss.

My parents met when my mother inherited an astonishing amount of money in 1969, after the sale of her family's estate in Cannes, France. The way my father tells it, "Sylvie floated into my office on the wings of cherubs and said, *'Bon Jour, I am in a terrible predicament, for I have a gazillion dollars, a tight concert schedule, the face of an angel, and the body of a goddess. Could you please help me?'"* Allegedly, Sylvie then fainted for no explicable reason. My father claims she fell into his arms, and he carried her to a chaise lounge in the dimly lit corner of his office. Sometimes, Dad throws something into the tall tale about the office being bathed in candlelight with rose petals scattered about the room. Anyway, rose petals or no, Dad maintains that he then kissed Sylvie passionately and pledged to protect her forever from sorcery, dragons, and the IRS.

Mother, at five feet eleven in her socks, always laughed at that story with such effervescent delight; I, on the other hand, believed his account to be accurate until I reached third grade. That was around the same time that I recall waking up one morning and shouting with horrid realization, "Oh, my God, Santa isn't real!" However, I neither hold my father culpable for his divisive yarns of young love nor for his stories of a fat man in a red suit flying through the Christmas sky via reindeer. My dad is too kind to accuse, too charming to doubt, and wholly innocent of the brutal murder of food critic Leonard Pruitt—the man who nearly destroyed me with a fabricated story of food poisoning, limp cilantro, and a one-star review.

Hors D'oeuvres

To: lancevega@freeme.org
From: honeyfried@honeycuttinc.com

July 10, 2013

Subject: Tom Honeycutt

Dear Lance,

    I know we have met on a few social occasions. My name is Clara Honeycutt, or Honey as I'm often called. My father, Tom, and your dad played tennis on occasion, and my dad served on the board of Free Me a few years ago. I was very sorry to hear of your father's passing. Please accept my condolences.

    Lance, I would like to meet with you. I am interested in your services. Of course, I am sure you know that almost a year ago, my father plead guilty to the murder of Leonard Pruitt. But I assure you, despite my father's confession, he did not commit this crime.

    Please, if you would be willing to meet with me, I know you would see, this is all a horrible mistake.

I look forward to hearing from you.

Sincerely,

Honey

"What in the actual hell?" My sister's shrill voice cracked with egomania and echoed off the kitchen walls in my parents' elaborate Upper West Side brownstone. My mother cooed and consoled her, which disgusted me.

"Marcella, *precious*," Mother pleaded. "Please, do not make this into a thing. Everything we are going through as a family..." Her voice crackled, and her French accent reared its lovely head through her cavernous sorrow. "Our family, we are all suffering. Everything is so difficult right now. *Please, dear.*"

I couldn't take much more of my older sister's despicable complaining. Her frenzy centered on a *discrepancy* that *People Magazine* made when they failed to mention *Marcella Monet*, my sister's "stage" name, in the cover story of the latest issue. The cover featured a dapper photograph of the late Leonard Pruitt. The insert photos, in the right-hand corner of the gossip rag's cover, featured my beloved dad in shackles as he was escorted from his sentencing hearing for Pruitt's violent murder. Included was a picture of me cutting the red ribbon of my now infamously doomed, once five-star restaurant, with the mayor of New York by my side.

"Why would they interview me and ask me all those questions?" Marcella screeched. "Why would they photograph me in my studio? Wasting my *irreplaceable* time and then not even mention *me!*"

Mother politely blew her nose Mother politely blew her nose in French. Dabbing her fine, creamy skin with her handkerchief, she kept trying her old tricks to dampen Marcella's latest drama with the same tired song and dance: *Poor Marcella. How can I make you happy?*

Contempt? Nah, I passed that emotion a long time ago. I suppose the word works, though. My sister and I keep a *contempt*uous relationship. Actually, I loathe her. She is oblivious to anyone but herself. Marcella and Honey. Like peanut butter and jelly. Only the peanut butter is a pompous ass, and the jelly is insubordinate and insists on being called Honey, even when the bee's nectar is most sour.

Marcella, the spitting image of my mother, inherited Sylvie's tall, willowy, jet-black hair and porcelain skin. In brash defiance of this, Marcella wears a super-short, bleach-blonde pixie cut. If I didn't know her, I would say, Marcella is stunningly beautiful like Mother. But I know Marcella very well, and beauty or no beauty, *she sucks.*

It'd be fair on your part to assume I am just jealous. The fact is, one could easily surmise that an immaculate conception took place when Tom and Sylvie Honeycutt birthed their daughters. It is as if the angel Gabriel himself zap-fried two bouncing baby girls: one with Sylvie's exclusive DNA, and the other (me) with only Tom's.

Dad's wiry, mouse-brown hair that had once sprung out from his scalp in tight round coils had completely vacated the premises. These days, he couldn't be any balder. Were it not for his white eyebrows, Dad easily could pass for a very Caucasian bowling ball. Still, I can honestly say, I am not jealous of Marcella because she looks like Mother and I favor Dad because I got Dad's beautiful, turquoise-blue eyes. And the wire-brush coil hair? I got that too, and I love my bouncy curls that sit atop my head in a wild display of tumbles and loops. I always keep them safely secured from food prep in a tight hair tie. Just don't come near me with a hairbrush, or all hell breaks loose. This is the Cardinal Rule of Curly Girl sisterhood: No Brushing.

Folks shy away from commenting on how closely I resemble Dad. Instead, they default to "Oh! You look just like the daughter from that sitcom! Darlene! From *Roseanne!*" This used to irritate me, but then I considered how I was being typecast as the actual Darlene in real life. In which case, no one would ever really know that I was not the sitcom character but someone else entirely. That line of thought only further exploits my lack of zeal for appearances. However, appearance is part of any experience. And nothing impacts appearance more than authentic quality. My dad always said, "*You can plate freezer-bought biscuits on China but the hand-rolled ones on a paper plate will tell the whole truth.*"

My sister only favors our mother's appearance; she has no other qualities I would compare.

Our mother's wonderful traits are many, including that of being generous to a fault. She is a woman who is kind, polite, and bashful. Unless she is performing on stage in front of thousands. Then she is a blinding light of bold excellence brandishing a violin, hypnotizing her audience like a magician or a witch.

Now, Marcella isn't selfish—just grossly self-obsessed. Maybe not a sociopath, but she could put a narcissist to shame. Which, since she has no talent or soul, is like pouring fine wine into a bottomless bucket. Nothing is ever enough. Not her five-million-dollar Manhattan condo with a view of the park. Not the financial freedom she carelessly and greedily sucks from our parents. Not the haven Mother and Dad have provided the woman's own children. Marcella is the quintessential succubus.

"Can't we sue them?" Marcella wept.

"Oh, my God," I spat. "You are *ridiculous!* I can't even ask how you could be so disgusting! None of this about you!" Which was the problem. All Marcella Jeanne Honeycutt cared about was herself.

"I hate you!" Marcella screamed. Yes, full-on screamed. Her fists balled, she stomped her red-bottom, Christian Louboutin-covered foot like a toddler in dress-up stilettos and *screamed*.

Mother float-rushed across the marble-tiled floor to Marcella's side, shooting me a foreboding yet stunning glare. I felt a catch in my chest. Even in her brokenness, she is ever breathtaking, flawless.

"*Marcella.*" Mother wrapped her arms around my wicked, full-blooded sister, and I felt a gag rising. "Baby, I will call the attorney and see if he can reach out to the magazine editor. Maybe they will feature your wonderful work separately? Wouldn't that be lovely?"

Marcella gushed, "Oh, Mummy! Thank you!" She hugged my mother, and, with Mother's back to me, stuck her tongue out at me. The woman is *thirty-four years old*. And since I am thirty-two, I flipped her off.

"Unbelievable," I said flatly and then yelped, *"You are a shit show, Marcella!"* I hopped off my stoop at the kitchen island and slipped on my Birkenstocks, unable to stay in my sister's nonsensical exosphere another second. I stormed from the kitchen, collecting my things in a fury to get as far from her as possible.

"Did you fight with Aunt Markie?" a small voice assaulted me, and I stopped just shy of the front door. Turning around, remorse rushed in a shudder up my spine.

"No, buddy." I moved in defeat to the sofa, where my eight-year-old nephew, "Davy," sat playing a video game. Exasperated, I flopped down next to him. "Just a disagreement."

David Honeycutt is one of two of my sister's illegitimate sons. Bo Honeycutt is the other. Bo is fifteen and *troubled*. Davy is perfection. My parents raised both boys as their own, and both of them call my sister *Aunt Markie*. Which Marcella hates, but my dad started the trend when Marcella did not want the boys to call her "Mommy." You know how some people don't like to be labeled. Although, in this instance, I agree with my *big sis*. She may have birthed the boys, but she is no one's mommy. I voted for something easy, like Beebe. Which, of course, would be short for *Beelzebub*.

Davy put the game remote down and snuggled into me. I squeezed his little body into my ample side, rubbing his round, crew-cut head. "It sounded really bad." Davy looked up at me, his beautiful brown eyes swimming in curiosity behind his Harry Potter-style glasses.

I playfully tugged on Davy's ear. "Well, you don't know anything. You're just a dumb kid. And you look like a tiny Will Smith." I poked his ribs, and he squirmed and howled. Which, yeah, made me choke back tears for the billionth time today. "Who's Will Smith?" Davy cackled.

I tickled his rib and quizzed, "*Men in Black*?"

"I can't watch that!" he argued. "It's got bad words in it!"

"Aww, you aren't so dumb after all," I cooed, kissing his soft, brown checks. "I take the dummy part back."

"I got a one hundred on my math test!" he bragged.

"Oh, my! I stand corrected. You are *very* smart."

Marcella strutted through the living room like an overzealous peacock, shooting me a triumphant grin. "Gotta bolt! Mummy has a call into a friend of a friend at the *New York Times* about a feature of *just me!*" The last part was barely audible as she slammed the front door behind her.

Davy's blameless voice reverberated her neglect. *"Bye, Aunt Markie."*

She was already gone.

Davy picked up his controller and started his game again. If he had simply grown used to his birth mother's neglect at that point in his life, I'd have hated Marcella even more. But I didn't believe Davy had grown numb to Marcella's abandonment. I heard the little dude trying to contain his sniffles... and failing. I cannot understand how she can be so cold. Davy's skin is a beautiful, golden-apple brown betty crisp color, and he is just as sweet.

Davy got his first pair of glasses when he was only eighteen months old. The child was already so darling without them, but in his navy-blue, Harry Potter-esque spectacles, with those big eyes magnified behind the coke bottle lenses, I could sop him up with a biscuit! He is absolutely the most beautiful, charming, sweetheart, angel baby that ever lived. If I didn't feel his warm body next to mine, I'd swear he was a character out of a Pixar movie.

"You okay, my man?" I nudged Davy.

"Yeah," he said, "I just miss Poppy." He wrinkled his nose, wide eyes on the television screen.

I was spent, but I couldn't contribute any more disappointment to this child's atmosphere. I inhaled some resolve as I pushed my canvas sack purse off the couch and picked up the second game controller. "Wanna get your butt kicked at Mario, dummy?"

Davy nodded, a small glimmer of "okay-ness" washing over his face. We played until my mother called him to dinner.

Upstairs, finally alone in my spacious flat, I cried. I cry all the time now. Since my dad confessed to the murder of Leonard Pruitt, and my restaurant went on "temporary" hiatus, I cry dozens of times a day. Which is not like me at all. Sometimes, the heartbreak and disbelief of this mess attack me like a rabid dog. Jumping out of the bushes, without warning, rushing at me with malnourished rage, intent on consumption. It is then, I am left in a heap of chaotic heartbreak that is so unlike me, I am shocked at my own reflection in the mirror. Once, I went so far as to look into my glistening eyes and sob out, "Is that you, Darlene? Is this a rejected episode of *Roseanne*?" But it is me; my dad's turquoise eyes staring back at me always remind me of that. And this mess is my life. Like so many nights since this nightmare began, and my dad's *confession*.

Why did he confess? I have asked myself this repeatedly.

This is how I spend my nights now, asking the same questions. *He confessed.* Dad is as gentle as a hand-embroidered throw pillow. And yet, *he confessed*. Every two weeks for the last nine months, our home manager and driver, Axel, has taken me to Attica, where I spend a lowly Sunday having the exact same conversation with my dad.

"How's Mom?"

"As well as can be expected."

"How are the boys?"

"Fine."

"When are you reopening the restaurant?"

Which is the point when I demand, *"Why did you confess? How can I help you? What in the actual hell is going on, Dad?"*

And Dad then shuts down and talks about the weather and how much he enjoys working in the prison library. By the time we say our goodbyes, my insides are boiling, and I can empathize with the rage that causes one human being to shoot another. I get it. I love my dad more than I love any other being, and the fact that he will not talk to me makes me feel like Freddy Kruger—murderous toward him. To which I reason, I could never kill my father because of the fact that he says things like, *"I most enjoy my time organizing the periodicals in the prison library."* When a year ago he was running a financial empire, managing my restaurant, chasing after his beloved grandsons, and drinking coffee on the porch while reading the paper.

Blood-boiling rage doesn't manifest due to reading a blurb in *The Post* discriminating against my restaurant. A multi-millionaire with a tri-weekly tennis appointment, followed by rowdy lunches at the club with a brotherhood of balding accountants, doesn't shoot a food critic in the head and dump his body in the Hudson over words. A paragraph of *typed*—sorry, untrue—out-of-character words. Words that barely made a ripple in the universe.

And it always comes back to this, the tears and the questions. I know no one ever believes that one of their own could be a monster.

They are crushed and *just had no idea*. But *I know my dad*. And even if he were not the person everyone thought they knew, I know he would never do anything to risk hurting his grandsons. No way. Dad would never hurt Bo and Davy.

Dragging myself through my little flat, I yanked open the refrigerator. The bright interior light alerted me to another foreign experience I still do not know how to process. *I have no appetite*. My therapist says it is a common issue, a post-traumatic stress response. Something else I do not understand. Normally, there is nothing I would rather do in lieu of eating. And not gross metric tons of greasy comfort food. Bites, luxurious tastes of contrasting textures and flavors, the exploration of aromas, noting temperature, consistency, and spice. This is passion to me. Romance, love, and sex are simply distractions, nothing I would go out of my way for. *Amoré* to me is a single jalapeño stuffed with my signature sausage, smoked cheddar, and Mascarpone, roasted on an open flame. The salad course would be a cooling journey of peppery arugula salad with peach vinaigrette and half-pickled Vidalia onions. Next, my chef-d'oeuvre, a succulent filet of blackened sea bass with avocado-cilantro aioli and a dusting of tossed almonds, with a side of hatch chili grits. Alas, none of it wets my whistle; none of it fills me as it did.

To be deprived of this relationship with food is a life sentence in and of itself. Jesus, help me! *I sound like Marcella*. I don't want to over-disclose it, and yet, food isn't my trade. It is my art. My friend. Similarly, my dad isn't just my dad and business partner. He is my friend.

Slamming the fridge closed, I continued to wander about my flat, straightening throw pillows while thinking of ways to stop thinking. Finally, with nothing left to straighten or fluff, I tend to my plants. Since Dad's conviction, my interior garden has thrived like never before. When my mother and I decided to close the restaurant *temporarily*, my plants bore the brunt of my apathy. I repotted twenty-five succulents. I trimmed

HORS D'OEUVRES

twelve Christmas cacti and started seven pothos ivy cuttings. All those little cuttings now sit in a variety of jars and vases in the bay window overlooking my parents' tiny green space behind our shared home.

I pour myself a glass of merlot and open the balcony doors. The evening air is dense with the remnants of summer sunshine, the sky rising gray, aglow with city night lights. My balcony offers no substantial view except for the lovely rooftop garden of the building behind us. I am obsessed with that little slice of city green. Other than that, I can see the back of the carriage house, where Axel Delgado, our family's home manager, lives a few feet behind the garage.

This space used to my dad's and my sanctuary. Now, it's just mine. I miss him and just can't seem to get past knowing, *He didn't do this*. He did not kill Leonard Pruitt. Giving into my perpetual disillusionment, I sat down on one of the two smooth, white, Adirondack chairs. The one to my right, my dad's "usual" seat, sits empty. I sipped wine, and my stomach growled at me, begrudging me and my grief-induced food aversion. I lay my head back and let the tears come *again*.

My mind drifted to one night, a mere nine months ago—the Thursday night before the grand opening of my new location. Dad and I had been at the restaurant since seven a.m. We'd only gone home at 3 a.m. for a couple of hours of sleep and a shower. It was now well past 10 p.m., and we still had hours of work to do. Dad walked past me in my kitchen, waving some papers, and piped, "Chef, I need you in the dining room to discuss the table setup."

I had mindlessly answered, "no."

Dad threw the papers he was carrying into the air and yelped, "*That is it! I quit!*" This fully alarmed my staff and left me with a knackered grin.

I shook my head and bantered back, "I fired you three times last week. You need to decide on the arrangement without me. I need to perfect the fish course." I squeezed more lime on a fresh piece of raw salmon.

Dad pulled a stainless pot off the rack over his head, swung it inches from my nose, and then pointed it at me like a weapon.

"Chef!" he yelped. "You will come with me to the dining room, or next time, I won't miss! You want me to put another bump in that crooked Honeycutt nose?"

A laugh escaped me. "No, sir."

"Good girl." He set the pot on the counter. "Get your butt in the dining room!"

I complacently nodded, wiping my citrus-glazed hands on my apron. I gave instructions to one of my assistants and followed Dad to the dining room.

Now, more tears trickled down my cheeks, and I squeezed my eyes tight, willing myself back to that night. *Rewind, rewind … rewind.*

The dining room had been dark, but when Dad flipped the switch, the room came alive with shouts of "Surprise!" Everyone I loved—well, and *Marcella*—was there to celebrate amid the madness. Dad had even invited the neighbors and a few old friends from culinary school. Pizza boxes were piled high, cases of cold beer and sodas were stacked, and an enormous cake with bright-yellow buttercream frosting that spelled out the words, Congratulations, Honey! sat on the table.

Davy ran to me, wrapping his little arms around my legs. "Happy birthday, Aunt Honey!" My mother tapped his shoulder and whispered something in my nephew's ear. "I mean," Davy stammered, "*comgrapulations* on your new place!"

I knelt and embraced him, and when I stood, Dad handed me a plate of greasy, decadent pizza and a cold beer.

He wrapped a thick, short arm around my shoulders. "Sorry about the nose wisecrack." Dad winked. "I figured I'd have to play dirty to get you out of the kitchen. I am so proud of you. Everything will be perfect. Let's celebrate in lieu of all else!" And he kissed me abruptly on the cheek, raised his beer, and said, "Thank you everyone for coming! Without each of you, our family would not have anything to celebrate. To more of this! To more, health, wealth, joy, and laughter! *To more everything!* Bon appetite, my friends!"

More everything. Dad always said that. I know he meant it. He is generous, and he just loves his people. Dad is the ultimate diplomat. Always offering a better, more generous idea with, "in lieu of…" suggestions. Which is a darling habit he picked up from my mother's French etiquette. Only Dad says it with a little bit of a drawl. Just a quiet, contemplative thought, usually followed by a silly Southern saying. He loved us. *He loves us.* And now, he is in prison. Every visit, the same desperate need to understand is left unquenched, and each time, Dad speaks with resolve and finality. Mother still has not gone to see him. She just breaks into heaving sobs if I even say "Dad."

Suddenly, another memory of that celebratory night, months ago, complained in my head, angry for attention: Mother and Dad fighting in a corner of the main dining room. I remembered, I had taken Davy to the bathroom, and as we made our way back to food and friends, I saw them. Mother was crying. Dad had his arms folded over his chest, an unfamiliar, pained scowl on his round face. I had quickly ushered Davy away. I had meant to ask Dad about it, but until this moment, I had forgotten.

I considered my mother and father and the unusual sighting of them at odds, and then a crash of trash cans in the alley jolted me from my evening dream. Bo, my fifteen-year-old nephew, was doing a poor job of *sneaking* over the back fence by the garage. He haphazardly threw his backpack over ahead of him. His school uniform was terribly wrinkled, his yellow-and-blue plaid tie dangling loosely around his shoulders.

"What are you doing?" I hollered down at him.

"Shit!" Bo yelped. "You scared the hell out of me!"

"I'm going to knock your block off if you cause Gram and Pop *any* grief."

"Yeah, yeah. Aunt Honey, can I come up?"

An hour later, Bo was laid out on my couch, full of an impromptu dinner of pan-fried venison, whipped turnips, and fried green beans. I concocted a creamy, honey-jalapeño ranch dip for the green beans, which Bo all but drank once the green beans were gone. I was only able to eat a few bites, finding the wine barely palatable; mostly, I picked at the artisan loaf of bread I had toasted in the broiler. But Bo had eaten every bit, followed by two root beer floats and a sleeve of Oreos.

I kind of cleaned up the kitchen, or pretended to, and Bo watched television. The show was some reality nonsense that made me queasy with its imposing melodrama. I pushed Bo's feet off the couch and sat. Bo moved his men's size-twelve feet back into my lap.

"Gag!" I plugged my nose, wincing. But then, nearly by habit, I began to rub my nephew's smelly feet, his loose, argyle socks slightly damp with sweat. As I tugged his socks up and rubbed his high arches, I recounted how tiny his feet had been the first time I held him. I love this child. I bit back more tears.

"Bo," I said, my voice strained. "I love you."

"Gross! Aunt Honey!" Bo leaped from the couch; his voice fractured with pubescence. "I thought you were a lesbian!" He slipped on his uniform loafers as I lay back on the couch in his spot.

"You're an idiot," I said smugly, resting my head on my folded hands. Then I teased, "I just wanted to lie down." Bo pulled my hair and flopped into my new, grass-green, velvet chair. When I am not crying or tending to my interior garden, I fill the void with impulsive furniture purchases.

"This chair sucks." He fidgeted. "Why is it shaped so stupid? Are you having a *Queer Eye* makeover in here?"

I sat up to look at him, grabbed a houndstooth throw pillow, and punched it twice before stuffing it under myself. I leaned on my elbow, admiring him. "It's retro. As in mid-century modern? It isn't meant to be comfortable. Comfort entices overstaying *your* welcome." I winked at him. "And I am not a lesbian. I'm just not interested."

Bo scoffed in disbelief. "*Everybody* is interested."

"Says the pimpled-faced teenage boy who carries a condom from health class in his wallet. Horny children and misogynists always believe *everyone is interested.*" I softened my tease. "You look good in that chair."

He laughed, laying his head back. The ease of Bo's presence assured an old, familiar feeling, and comfort gathered with us, just for a moment. With the warm scent of *boy feet* and venison steak still lingering in the air, Bo smirked and declared, "I look good in anything."

"The curse of the Honeycutts," I volleyed. But I noticed Bo flinched a bit and then didn't move. His chiseled, pimpled jaw tightened. Bo is stunningly handsome, with olive skin and forest-green eyes subtly flecked with gold. His curly, rusty auburn hair is an exotic mystery. The boy's wild mane has been a battle since he was two, but it is charming, nonetheless. I didn't want to cry again. I don't know if loving children as I love Bo and Davy is the same as motherhood. But, if it is even a dollop as much, I cannot imagine loving more intensely.

Bo spoke into the quiet, "But I'm not a Honeycutt. I'm not anyone."

My insides leaped up from the couch to correct him. But my weary body just sank into the sofa.

"Don't be a jackass, Bo," I piped. I know, that sounds like I am the worst. I probably am. But we tease. We used to tease anyway. I want us to be like we used to be before my dad was so horrifically ripped from our lives. I continued, "You *are* a Honeycutt. You cannot get rid of us."

With a huff, Bo moved to stand, slinging his backpack over his shoulder. "Not like I'd have anywhere else to go anyway. My *mother* is such a whore, my birth father is probably some homeless dude she screwed on the subway." I sat up. Before I could speak, Bo said, "I gotta go. I have a chemistry quiz to make cheats notes for. Thanks for the food."

I followed Bo to the door that leads from my flat to the family residence.

"Hey." I reached up to tug on my nephew's ear. Among the things I cannot get used to: Looking up at this man-child and tiptoeing to kiss his handsome cheek. "*We* are Honeycutts. And we are gonna be okay." Bo and I embraced, and he relaxed, then tightened the embrace, holding me for longer than either of us was accustomed to. "I love you, Bo."

He inhaled and pulled from me. "I still think you are a lesbian."

"I still think you are an idiot. Now get out of here." And I swatted at his bottom. "Cheat your best!"

Bo took two quick steps down and turned. "Aunt Honey!"

His yelp stopped me just as I closed the door. "What?"

"Can I ask you something?" His face morphed, and serious concern showed in his plea.

"Of course, you can come to me with anything. You know that," I said, gently punching him in the shoulder.

"Yeah." Bo nodded. He held his stare, and I braced myself, desperate to help him, afraid of what he might ask. Finally, Bo asked, "Aunt Honey, how'd you know about the condom in my wallet from health class?" And he menacingly flashed his trademark, wicked grin.

"Get off my stoop, ya nasty brat!" I slammed the door, still howling-laughing at my nephew's wit and cutting humor… and then I burst into tears.

HORS D'OEUVRES

It was time to stop pretending. I poured the rest of the bottle of wine into a plastic tumbler and guzzled it while standing over the sink, leaving all but one more swallow. Then I grabbed a prescription bottle out of the cupboard and, against the advice of my doctor or any other sane person, took two sleeping pills.

I slept peacefully through fifteen hours of blood-soaked night terrors, void of tossing and turning, in lieu of grieving.

Amuse-Bouche

Rat-a-tat-tat.
    Rat-a-tat-tat.

The bashing rattle persisted and finally nagged me from my intoxicated slumber. My head was either pounding so hard my teeth were rattling or someone was at the door, or both.

I yelped, "*Just a sec!*"

Peeking out of my bedroom door, I could see Axel Delgado standing on my balcony. Axel is our family's, well… Axel does everything. The man once worked as a hotel manager for some swanky hotel in Buenos Aires. Ten years ago, my parents were staying in Argentina for a meeting about a property investment, and Axel dazzled Mother and Dad. Highly impressed with the way he ran the hotel, interacted with guests, and his overall presence, they begged him to come to work for them in New York. A naturally dynamic aura emanated from the man. His skin shined in a rich caramel tone tinged with generous portions of butter and molasses. His velvety brown eyes, sharp features, long-angled nose, and full rouge lips made him all the more striking. Aged thirty-nine, he wore his shiny black hair in a trim, clean-cut style befitting his years. His facial hair, a combo of dark, serious eyebrows and barely-there goatee, would, one might think, be enough to draw a few stares. However, it's his stature that catches everyone's eye. Axel is six-two and built like a tank. He isn't overly muscular; just *very* fit. The natural body shape for a professional soccer player, and that had been the rung he'd been reaching for—until he blew out his knee and was forced into a new career. But Axel remains diligent in his wellness pursuits, which often lends to his attempts at force-feeding me apples or prodding me to go for a run.

The latter of which will never, ever happen.

Mother and Dad invited Axel to come to the United States, offering him ten times his salary at the hotel in Argentina. They helped him migrate to New York and become a citizen. His duties include *everything*. Axel bears the titles of business manager, bodyguard, courier, errand boy, peacekeeper, and babysitter… and then some. Axel actually delivered Davy in the back seat of our family sedan.

That is one of Marcella's least favorite stories. So, I tell it often. Pregnant yet again, with no clue who the father is, Marcella scheduled a C-section, immediately followed by a tummy tuck in Los Angeles. My sister often travels to LA—her hotspot to rehabilitate, undergo plastic surgery, or hide from the New York social scene while calving her illegitimate sons.

However, Marcella had left for California before Davy was born give birth and then repair the damage done while fulfilling her duty—in her mind, the "consequences" of a drunken sleepover—and forgot to sign a waiver of intent that would have allowed my parents to take the baby from the hospital. This would ultimately prevent Mother and Dad from returning to New York, immediately after the birth, as the child's permanent legal guardians. The documents had to be completed in New York, so Marcella flew back home. She signed the papers and, an hour later, was headed back to the airport.

The short version of the story is, Davy is a New Yorker. Marcella blamed the entire calamity on Axel, claiming that he was culpable for the papers not being signed. She threatened to sue him for the tear in her perineum—something about delivering the head wrong and not driving fast enough or hitting a pothole. Marcella's claim: The baby's head and Axel's incompetency messed up her lady parts. My dad wouldn't fire Axel or sick the legal team on him. So, Marcella pouted in California for a year, neither visiting Davy nor even inquiring about the beautiful baby boy. While in the City of Angels, she had a breast lift, a tummy tuck, got a designer vagina, and had her tubes tied. The universe relaxed after that procedure, recognizing the idiocy of creating my sister fertile.

I pulled on my fuzzy green robe, barely glanced in the mirror, and rushed to the door.

"Morning," I yawned. "Sorry, I—"

"Self-medicated," Axel finished for me, nodding toward the empty wine bottle and burgundy-stained glass on the counter.

"Funny," I said shortly, stepping aside to let him through the door. "What time is it?"

"Ten-fifteen."

Axel didn't say it accusingly, but I apologized anyway. "Oh, gosh, I'm so sorry. Was I supposed to meet you?"

Axel began cleaning up the rest of my cooking frenzy from the night before, ignoring my question. He then admonished me with his exaggerated and highly aggressive washing of the wine glass. After finishing that exercise, he forebodingly shot me a glare as he sniffed the tumbler I left sitting next to the empty bottle of wine. He picked up the prescription bottle and shook it at me. I tried to mentally count how many pills rattled.

"You aren't taking these with alcohol, are you?" he asked, his Latin accent sharp with rolling consonants.

I flopped onto the couch, pretending I didn't hear him. The loud clang of him dropping the wine bottle into the recycling container made me shudder. I rubbed my temples, letting Axel go about his business of… whatever this intrusion was about. I felt a cold, wet smack and looked up to see Axel standing over me.

"What was that?" I asked with indignation.

"It's a wet rag. Wash that crust off your face."

I begrudgingly followed his instructions, my hands itching from the invasion. Then he handed me a small glass of tomato juice and a handful of Advil.

"Thanks," I remarked out of polite obligation only, vexed that Axel was treating me like a child.

He sat down in my new green chair. "This is a terrible chair. I told you it was a mistake."

I gulped down three blue pills, willing them to stop the incessant pounding in my head while simultaneously begging the tomato juice to go down *and stay down.*

"It's not a mistake. It looks beautiful. It isn't meant to be comfortable. It is meant to be stylish."

He snorted. "Have you sat in it?"

"When I bought it, yes. But, no, not since."

"Why not?"

"It's not comfortable. I like the couch."

Once again, he let out a snort. "Well, anything is comfortable when you're passed out cold."

"Please don't lecture me, Axel. You aren't my dad." Which, of course, choked me up. But I wasn't going to fall apart before lunch. I had a schedule: *Fall apart in hysterics—2:00 p.m.* in my trusty day planner. Had Axel the miraculous house man not come banging on the door, I could have easily slept the day away.

"What do you want anyway?" It came out uglier than I had intended but was spot-on for how I felt.

"Your mother has been trying to reach you. Bo didn't show up to school. She's worried about him *and you*."

"Did you take him to school?"

Axel shot me a glare. "No. He wanted to walk with friends."

I stood and walked to the bedroom, where I grabbed my phone off the nightstand. Twelve texts from my mother and one from Bo's first-period teacher.

I returned to the living room to find Axel on the couch now. I sat in the uncomfortable yet stylish green chair with a humph.

"You should get dressed. We can go look for him," Axel suggested, downing the coffee from his insulated cup.

"He's fine." My thumbs quickened as I sent a text to Mother: *I'm fine, just overslept, don't worry about Bo. I will find him.*

I didn't look up from my phone but said to Axel flatly, "There is no point in chasing him. I will take care of it."

Axel rose in a swift movement, notably irritated. "Yeah, I figured. *You'll take care of it*. Meaning, you'll let Bo do whatever he wants as long as you get to wallow in self-pity and Bo ends up here to ward off your loneliness, encouraged to be a rebellious ass by his infamous *Aunt Honey*. He doesn't need a buddy! He needs direction. *A parent*."

"God, you are so pious. And I am not Bo's mother." I pulled a gagging face, and Axel stormed around the kitchen and began to open cabinets.

"What are you doing?" I snapped.

"Making some coffee."

"I don't want coffee."

"I do," he chipped back at me.

I bit back a real gag now, both in irritation and because, Lord, I was not sure whether I could stomach the smell of brewing coffee. I miss coffee, but maybe I merely long for the idea of it. The familiar ritual of that first morning sip. Or perhaps it was the persistent memories of the gallons Dad and I drank together, huddled around the kitchen island of my flat or sitting on the balcony. Since the wheels fell off my life, I can barely tolerate the smell of coffee. And the taste? My tongue registers nothing. It just feels warm and thick.

So now, the casual proposition of coffee, once as refreshing to my soul as a babbling freshwater brook would be to a castaway on a deserted isle, makes me wretch, my tastebuds repulsed by the mere suggestion of that hot, creamy, and once-sweet decadence.

"Are you sure you don't want some?" Axel pressed.

I ignored him—*Axel knows I can't drink coffee*—and typed a message out to Bo: *BO, what the hell? I don't need this. Where are you?*

I slipped the phone into the pocket of my robe and then muttered, "I'm going to need the car. Apparently, you will make yourself at home. I'm going to shower. You can let yourself out."

Axel snorted. "I'll wait. You aren't driving. It's not safe with all those chemicals in your system."

I slammed the bathroom door, meant as an emotional blow to my unwelcomed flat guest, but the Advil hadn't started working, so I only punished myself. Bracing myself on the sink, I leaned in close to the mirror. My eyes began to well up, and salty, wine-enriched tears rolled down my plump cheeks. My hazy, wet gaze, along with Axel's incessant banging around in *my kitchen*, was going to make it hard to stay on task. I turned on the shower, the hot water on full blast, and relished in the semi-seclusion as steam began to billow in the tiny, nearly stark-white space of my bathroom.

As I pulled off my clothes, I reveled in the privacy and the bright white of my little bathroom—one of my favorite spaces that my mother and I created when we remodeled the attic, transforming it into my flat. We spent hours combing through designer magazines and Pinterest, then designing and decorating together, until the space had morphed into a picturesque home of white subway and penny tile, brass fixtures, mid-century pops of furniture, and bold, top-of-the-line chrome appliances. The only other colors are occasional appearances of black-and-white houndstooth prints, bursts of green velvet—chosen by me—and my plants, of course. The flat, an open floor plan with bright, natural light and dark-wood maple floors, offers only one set of exterior doors, leading to my balcony and granting access to the backyard, carriage house, and garage. The single interior door leads to the stairs down to my parents' kitchen area. I adore my little space. And although, as of late, music has not been soothing, I decide to turn my shower radio up full blast to drown out my unwelcome, noisy guest.

I let the hot water run over me and began to co-wash my curls with some lavender-scented conditioner. The All 80s, All the Time station crooned Bananarama as I scrubbed and scoured. Then a rapid knock startled me out of my sudsy jam session.

"What?" I screeched.

"Better speed it up," Axel hollered. "Bo's been arrested."

"Shit!" I whisper-barked, rushing through a rinse. I bolted from the bathroom, a fresh white bath towel swaddled modestly around me, barking orders at Axel. "Go pull the car around! I will meet you in front in ten! And text Mom—tell her we are on our way!" I heard the patio door shut and felt a wave of relief, followed by a gush of anxiety and despair that could not be ignored.

Axel only texted twice, begging me to hurry. I cried for about fifteen minutes before I could get out of the apartment. I have found that if I pinch off a breakdown, it only magnifies the issue. I used the last of the Visine eye drops, then texted Axel: *pharmacy eye drops... be right down.* He texted back: *hurry your mother is freaking out that we haven't gotten Bo back.*

I climbed in the front seat of the Sedan, and Axel handed me a brown paper bag.

"Eye drops," he said flatly.

"How'd you get them so fast?" I questioned.

He snorted. "You texted me that request yesterday."

I huffed down in my seat, not longing to be lectured. But the silence crept on unbroken. So, I pulled my phone out and texted my therapist. *Need emergency appointment. After 1 pm please.* Then I folded my arms, turning away from Axel so as not to encourage his scolding.

Finally, my phone alerted me, breaking the monotony of not being reprimanded for self-medicating. And, unfortunately, because Axel is so embedded in my business, he got the confirmation for my counseling appointment at the exact same time I did.

I huffed audibly. Axel snickered, and I ignored him. Finally, I picked his driver's hat up off the seat.

"Why do you even wear this?" I asked lightly.

"Your dad and I thought it best I look the role of a driver. Not a bodyguard/errand boy/secretary. Appearances, I guess."

I started to fume. How dare Axel suggest my dad put on airs for anyone? My dad was not pretentious or fake or phony. Axel was just being an ass.

Axel spoke, "Honey, you remember about tonight, right?" His was tone softer now and more in need, so I dropped the hat on the seat. *He called me Honey.* That meant no lecture, and I was back in the driver's seat. Metaphorically speaking, of course.

I opened the calendar on my phone: *Dinner 7:00 Capital Grille: Axel's Cousin.*

"Yes. Of course," I promised.

"I must pick Diego and his wife, Valentina, up from JFK at five. So, I need to get you home from the counselor and then bolt. I don't know if I can make it back to pick you up before our reservation at seven o'clock."

"No problem," I assured him. "I can just get a cab."

"Okay, that would be great. But with traffic—"

I cut him off. "It won't be a problem. I will head out at six."

This time, a big grin spread across his face.

"Cool." Axel smiled and nodded. "This is a huge relief to me, Honey. I don't want to have to get into the whole mess about Tom…" He cut himself off just as we pulled into the police parking complex.

A few hours later, I flopped onto my therapist's plush, mustard-yellow sofa. Relief washed over me as I inhaled the aromas of lemongrass and rose essential oil. I basked in the privacy of the deep navy walls. The polished oak bookshelves lining the walls were filled with cerebral books, awards, and fake ivies. In Raven Cantu's office, I get to just let go. I can talk to Axel, mostly. He is my friend, but there is a fine line with him. He tends to get too friendly and forget he works for us. And then I tend to get too friendly and then feel awkward treating him like an employee. And I cannot talk to my mother; she is too fragile. And she is markedly averse to discussing any promises of a defense for Dad. In some ways, she nearly seems resolved. In the beginning, I thought it was shock. But lately, I've noticed that *if* Mother even speaks of my dad, it is in the past tense. Which only leaves my sister who, of course, I can't talk to because she is a jackass. My dad was my one true friend and confidant. But when I come to an appointment at Raven's, I don't get the same mundane answers, and I never feel patronized. I can just talk. And then she says something beautiful and wise, and I can trudge on with my life for a hot second.

The heavy oak door opened, and Raven glided into the office, her jet-black, silver-beaded dreadlocks clicking in tandem with the sway of her magical stride. Her skirt, a patchwork of brightly colored silk, each patch printed with a different, gold-stamped traditional Indian design. Her blouse, a breathy neon green that made me mentally begin crafting a key lime pie. I admire everything about Raven. She is wise and funny. I don't wish to be like other people. I wish to be *better* than other people, and most of the time, I believe I am. But if I had to pick a role model, it would be Raven Cantu.

Of course, she is old enough to be my mother, but she has an agelessness about her. Her dark skin is flawless, and her long, natural lashes flutter like a child's when she asks questions. Her golden eyes always seem to be conveying the message, *I know the answer, and so do you.* But her fluttering lashes and smooth cheeks, with what appear to be intentionally placed laugh lines, take the edge off her stern, knowing looks. My favorite part of Raven's appearance is her huge, wide smile, which reveals that big gap between her two front teeth. It is just the most endearing and authentically beautiful characteristic I have ever witnessed on another human being.

"Hey, Honey," Raven greeted me.

"Hey."

"So…" She folded her hands on her desk. "What's going on?"

The next forty minutes were a blur of hysterics. Me blubbering tales of Bo getting nabbed for shoplifting. Axel's bossy behavior, Marcella's tantrums, Mother's silence, and all things *Dad, Dad, and Dad.*

After I'd finished, Raven stood, walked toward me, and sat in a red wing-back chair covered in huge yellow roses. The chair, which I would

IN LIEU OF EATING

normally find aggressively optimistic, matched Raven's eclectic flare. I inhaled deeply, bracing myself for her life-giving encouragement.

"Honey," Raven purred, "I want you to listen to me. What I am going to say to you is important."

I nodded, certain I was looking wide-eyed and desperate.

"Honey, you are at a crossroads. Your dad confessed to this crime. He is in prison. He is not getting out. You are too young to live the life you are living, both in tragedy and complacency."

Wait. What is happening? I couldn't even form words. This is not the natural order or routine that I am used to. I continued to panic, but Raven appeared resolute.

Raven scooted forward in her seat and placed her long, jeweled hand on my knee, her bangled wrist clanking.

"It has been four years since you first began coming to me. It has been almost a year since your father went to prison. If he had passed away, we would have moved through the stages of grief. We would have set goals. We would have progressed. I cannot help you anymore."

"*What?*" I gasped.

She leaned back, clasping her hands together, and continued with her delivery. "Clara, I cannot in good conscience continue to tell you the dangers of self-medicating with alcohol, antidepressants, and sleeping pills."

Even if I could have spoken, I wouldn't have admitted, "*And Xanax.*"

Raven continued. "You need medical and psychiatric help, Clara. You can't come here and casually mention that Axel is on your nerves and reprimanded you for drinking and drugging and then expect me to say, *I wish you wouldn't do that. Tsk, tsk.*" She stopped as if to let me speak, but before I could, she continued. "I have referred you back to your primary care provider and told her what you are doing and asked her to help you find a psychiatrist that will work with your doctor. I care about you. I want you to have a full and beautiful life, and I will not stand by and talk circles around your current choices. My *life* advice is not helpful to you anymore."

Tears rolled down my face, soaking my somewhat sweaty blouse. She handed me a box of Kleenex, and I begrudgingly snatched at two tissues and then blew my nose loudly without apology.

Again, she leaned forward, clasping her hands together.

"Honey…" Her voice was soft. "…you are all about order and control. You are a genius with spices and specific ingredients." She tapped her fingers together, causing her bangled wrist to chime a mistimed, lighthearted melody. "I suspect you even control your senses."

I looked at her curiously and she continued, "You hate Chinese food but love Korean food. You tinker with Chinese dishes and try and make them more Korean or Thai. That is control, control you have mastered, but why? Why do you hate Chinese food?"

I thought for a minute and then said, "I just think the flavors are drab. Well, and…" I stumbled. "It's Marcella's favorite. We always had to go to this crappy dive in Brooklyn for her birthday…"

Raven touched my knee. "Stop. So Chinese food is not good enough until you make it do what you want it to do and disassociate it from your sister. Perfect example. Your hate for your sister has grown worse since we first met. And you can't control her or how you feel about her. Just like you can't control your dad's situation or how you feel about him. Round and round we go, and in my care, you have become a drug-dependent alcoholic. You don't need talk therapy, girl. You need a lobotomy."

She leaned back again casually, and her breathy voice calmly went on, "What good is it, Clara, to come here and grieve if you do not leave here and live?"

I shook my head aggressively. "I don't remember how?" I sniffled and whimpered. "My goals were to be the best chef. To make my parents proud. I don't know what to do with myself. All I cared about was my success." Now I was ready to beg. "Raven, can't you help me figure out what to do next?"

"No." She dropped her head, nearly shamefully. "Perhaps if we had just met and that was the goal for our work together, but, Clara, you do not need a life clinician, talk therapy, more supplements, different essential oils, or a reminder from me to breathe deeper and meditate, you need a doctor. You are not only continuing to stay in the same grips that have held you captive for a long time, but you are also creating new ones. Are you understanding me, Clara?"

I snorted and she stood and went to sit behind her desk.

"I will make this easy for you. I am about to piss you off." She wrote on a piece of paper for quite a while and then spoke again. "Don't read this until you get in the car. We are out of time. I am not rescheduling you. And I have sent an email to your family physician. She has already responded, and her receptionist is going to call you this afternoon. This can't be ignored, Clara." She stood and handed me a blue, folded piece of stationary, placed her hand on my shoulder, and said, "Get some help, Honey. *Please*." She left, shutting the office door behind her.

Outside the building, I texted Axel: *Come get me.*

He answered immediately: *you'll have to grab a cab, your mom needs me. See you tonight.*

I wandered to a bench under the shade of some mysterious tree and sat. I stared at the folded note unable to imagine how everything—including even Raven—was oozing out of my control. The summer sun reflected off the sidewalk, and I winced at the glare. I was stuck here on this bench until I could find a cab, so I unfolded the note and read.

Clara, I believe your father did kill Leonard Pruitt. He confessed. You must move on. You have the resources to build a new life, with or without your father—regardless of his guilt or innocence, no matter what you think you know about him. The life you can build can only fill you when it is built around you. You can only know yourself wholly. Know her, know Clara Honeycutt. Stop blaming, drinking, medicating, and hating. Get to know Clara. Notice what you love, in lieu of all that you blame. I wish you every bit of joy and wellness - Raven

Fury ravaged me. My dad *did not* kill Leonard Pruitt! And all these months I really believed that Raven of all people understood this. I wadded the note into a ball and stormed through the office greenspace in search of a trashcan. Nausea grabbed at my empty stomach. I hate being told what to do. Even when it is logical and sound. I quickly tossed the note from Raven in the trash and headed north toward Central Park in the hope of finding somewhere to get a drink to steady myself. I walked a few blocks and finally spotted an open-air Chinese food restaurant, cringed, and walked to the kiosk to ask for a table.

Under the shade of the shabby little diner's red awning, I flopped into a chair. I neglected pleasantries when a waiter swooped in and inquired, "Do you have a bar?"

"Yes, yes." The young waiter bowed. "Full bar. Can I get you something cold?"

"Yes, thank you. I'll have a Mai Tai, extra ice, double shot of dark rum on top, no fruit."

"Any food, ma'am?" he begged.

"Sure, some miso broth, and do you have a vegetable dim sung?"

"Yes, yes." The waiter bowed again. "I'll be right back."

I figured the miso would count as a protein, and I could pick the fluffy bread off the dumpling and call it lunch and dinner. As I drowned my second Mai Tai and felt the coconut-flavored rum vibrate in my veins, I realized I wasn't sad about Raven. Just pissed. The waiter set a third drink down, and I tried to do the math in my head regarding the number of shots I had just swallowed. My head was pounding, unreasonable rage tightening like a heavy hand around my throat. How dare Raven say she thought my dad killed Pruitt? Was everyone in my life going completely mad? I tore at the paper placemat, barely acknowledging the Chinese horoscopes. And then I quickly had a memory of Marcella joyfully reading everyone's Chinese zodiac signs as part of her traditional birthday ritual at her favorite Chinese restaurant.

With a trembling hand, I picked up the cold concoction in front of me and gulped, smirking. I am at a *Chinese food restaurant, Raven*, I thought. *And I am just fine. I don't need you anyway.*

Upon finishing the third drink, most of the miso broth, and all the bread off the dim sung, I steadied myself to stand, only to find I was too drunk. I flopped back down and looked at my iPhone: 3:22 p.m. And my phone battery was at 15 percent.

The young waiter showed up, a look of concern on his face. "Are you okay, ma'am?"

"Yes," I lied. "Yes, could I have a cup of green tea and a bowl of white rice?"

The waiter nodded, looking relieved that I was not about to drink and walk. And after two cups of green tea and four entire bites of rice that was way overcooked, I felt I had my sea legs. Still, I decided to wait a beat before heading out onto the street. I risked the last of my phone battery and started to mindlessly scroll through my phone. Habitually, I clicked on the first article saved, even though I have it memorized.

Leonard Mason Pruitt, aged sixty-three, was found murdered on Tuesday, October 25, 2012.

Pruitt was an accomplished author, chef, and food critic. He was the chief editorial food critic at The Post. *Leonard will be sorely missed by his colleagues and friends. In his spare time, Leonard Pruitt was the proud owner and trainer of his Irish Setter, grand champion gold cup winner Sir Caoimhin.*

Mr. Pruitt is preceded in death by his parents, Wallace and Esmeralda Imogene Pruitt. He is survived by his beloved daughter, Esmeralda Imogene "Emo" Pruitt. Leonard also leaves behind his fiancé, Tess Lambert. Condolences may be sent to The Post c/o Leonard Pruitt. In lieu of flowers, the family asks that a donation be made to the Alzheimer's Research Foundation, where Mr. Pruitt served diligently on the board in honor of his late mother, Imogene.

Emo Pruitt's name caught my attention this time, not that it hadn't in the months before. But today, in the fog of rum and rice, I considered her.

Emo Pruitt.

I wondered about her nickname. Of course, my dad called me Honey and Marcella, Markie. I wondered if Emo's dad had coined the nickname in her childhood or if it had been an intentional play on her maternal grandmother's name at the time of her birth. Regardless, I had only ever truly considered what I knew of Emo Pruitt prior to Leonard's death. Emo is a successful singer, songwriter, poet, artist, and business extraordinaire. She owns *Purple*, a gallery that doubles as a speakeasy on random nights, with a secret entrance behind one of her brightly-purple-colored abstract paintings.

Purple, a swanky, hidden gem in the West Village, promotes local artists who take a quarter of the club's evening's cut on the night of their performance. The speakeasy only serves 150 patrons at $1,000 cover per person, not including the bar, which is not included in the evening's 25-percent take. Any way you look at it, Emo Pruitt is a business mad genius. Artists clamor to be highlighted there, both for the coin and the exposure. And patrons are not only willing to pay the cover, but rumor also has it, she is booked solid through 2045. She doesn't even have a promise of being open, and New York is willing to pay and wait.

I clicked on another link and read.

Purple has been closed since the murder of gallery/club owner, Emo Pruitt's father, best-selling author and food critic Leonard Pruitt. When we reached out to Pruitt about a possible reopening, her publicist, Clover Mathis, said, "When it is open, it is open. In the meantime, Emo asks that you make contributions to non-profit art establishments that encourage, support, and promote young artists."

Admirable, I thought.

Intrigued, I trolled Emo on social media, noting her scarcity since November when her father died. But then, amid the hundreds of condolences, about six rows from the top, I saw it.

Leonard. The image of him, his dark skin, shiny with delighted pride, sucked the wind from me. The whites of his dark eyes and the huge smile on his face were exaggerated by his decadent, South African skin. Wrapped in his long, strong arms was a lanky woman with the same bright smile and dark eyes, but her skin was not as ebony; it was creamier, milk-chocolatey. Emo Pruitt. She is instantly recognizable. Emo wears her natural hair in a perfectly coifed gold-blonde afro. Which only highlights her sleek beauty. She is always seen wearing enormous gold hoop earrings and a variety of chokers lining her slim neck. Her wide smile enhances her chiseled jawline. She wears no makeup except for bold, matte-red lipstick. The minimalist blast of fiery scarlet perfectly enhances her natural beauty, making her nearly look fake. My dad's voice rattled in my head, the words he said to my mother daily, *"So pretty, you're too good to be true. I'd look at you in lieu of breathing."*

I stared at the pair, Leonard and his daughter, *Emo*, and immediately felt the vomit rising in my throat.

Still, I clicked on the caption and read.

My dad. My biggest fan. I will miss your hugs forever. I will practice your company in every moment. I love you, always.

And... I threw up rice and rum in my lap, in lieu of graciousness.

Soup

At 4:42, after cleaning up, apologizing profusely, tipping generously, and promising to never return to Hong's House of Hunan, I wandered into the park. Lucky for me, Hong's was next to a souvenir shop, so I bought an *I Love NYC* t-shirt, stepped into a side alley, and changed my vomit-laced blouse, dumping it into a nearby dumpster. None of this is an out-of-the-ordinary sighting in New York; I hardly blushed.

I walked with my canvas bag thrown over my shoulder and my phone clinging to a 2-percent charge. My Birkenstocks felt sticky, and the steaming heat of the city twisted and tightened the sweaty curls into coils on my damp neck. I felt...*miserable*. What was I even doing with my life? Waiting to wake up from this nightmare? Surely, there was something I could do. Granted, I had a meeting with an attorney, Lance Vega, tomorrow, but I was tired of hearing myself say, "My dad didn't kill Leonard Pruitt." I imagined everyone I encountered was tired of hearing it as well.

Out of the corner of my eye, I saw a big red dog chase across the park after a blue rubber ball, and a woman laughed and clapped. "*Good boy! That's a good boy, Kevin!" I snorted to myself; a dog named *Kevin*. But then I looked toward the dog's owner and immediately recognized her. As if the cosmos were contriving against me, I gasped and gagged just a little.

Emo Pruitt.

I stood staring in utter shock and then quickly ducked behind a tree. I was certain she would recognize me and was terrified of what she would say when she did. I continued to watch. Kevin the dog caught the ball mid-bounce and raced back to Emo. She laughed and clapped and repeated the process.

Emo Pruitt didn't look like she was inching up past thirty-five, but I remembered that she had graduated from NYU before Marcella. I chewed on my lip, questioning my reasoning. But then I quickly connected some sorority associations Marcella and Emo had.

I immediately realized the awkwardness of me spying on Emo, but it was like spotting some exotic animal in the wild. She was like a gazelle in Central Park. Her skin was taut and glowed. She wore tan, linen, wide-legged pants and a rich, raspberry-colored, flouncy tank top. Her sharp cheekbones glimmered in the afternoon sun, and her laugh reverberated in my bones. She looked and performed like a healthy, happy, beautifully *sane* person.

Either the rum or the tragedy confused me. Why was Emo laughing? Why was she throwing a ball to a dog named Kevin in the park? Why wasn't she like me—totally destroyed? Her dad was dead. My dad was in prison for killing her dad, and yet... Here was this statuesque woman playing fetch in the park with a dog named Kevin.

I attempted to be stealth-like and moved to a bench behind the duo to sit out of her sightline. I picked up my phone as the tiny Apple icon faded, giving up the illusion of a charge. Emo and Kevin continued to play. After seven or eight more ball tosses, Emo knelt and attached a bright blue leash to Kevin's collar. She guided the dog over to a khaki backpack under a tree and pulled out a black-and-yellow plaid blanket. Emo laid out the blanket and methodically folded her long legs under her to sit, simultaneously kicking off her sandals. Kevin lay next to her as she leaned back on the tree and drank from a large, metal water bottle. I watched as she closed her eyes, inhaling deeply and smiling.

The last of my stomach bile rose in my throat, burning it further. What was she smiling about? Was she on drugs? I watched as Emo's hand moved slowly over the dog's coat, and Kevin's eyes drifted shut. The sun barely moved; neither did she, that smile never leaving her face as she basked in the shade.

Finally, Kevin the dog began to stir, and Emo began packing up her things. I was paralyzed to move, entranced by this seemingly normal woman who I knew was living a life far from normal. Emo flung the backpack over her shoulder, adjusted the dog's lead on her slim wrist, and then started to walk toward the north entrance of the park. I watched her intently and felt a twinge of jealousy as she smiled at passersby. My insides screamed and squirmed. *Why are you okay?*

When I could no longer see Emo or Kevin, I dropped my face in my hands and let the tears come. They were shed quietly but could not be held back. I wanted to be okay. I did not want a dog in New York City, but I wanted to feel that other woman's contentment. Tears mingled with the sweat dripping off my brow, and I sunk further onto the park bench. I wished I could zap-fry myself back home in my little flat and will everything back to normal. Instead, there I was, stalking a victim's daughter in the park in a tourist's t-shirt. My throat dry and my tongue thick with stomach acid and stale rum, I resolved to die on the bench. If someone came looking for me, fine. Otherwise, I would just get lost among the homeless. Another washed-up chef on the streets of New York.

"Clara?" A voice from behind me broke through the crazy. "Clara Honeycutt?"

I kept my head down, rifling through my bag for a Kleenex. I found a ratty old tissue among dozens of its equally ratty brethren and then blew my nose, wiped my face, and turned.

"Yes?" I stopped. It was her. Emo Pruitt. "Oh. I, uh…" I had no excuse.

"I thought that was you. Were you watching me?" Her tone held lighthearted concern, not offense.

"No!" I answered too quickly and then lowered my overly enthusiastic opposition. "No, I mean, not on purpose. I was walking in the park and sat down and—"

She cut me off. "Thought you would spy on me?" Emo folded her arms across her trim body. A quizzical eyebrow raised, and I noticed how much her eyes looked like her father's.

"No, really. It was just an accident."

She tapped her foot, and a beautiful smile spread across her face. "I'm just kidding." And she laughed. The sound was warm and genuine and further confused me. "It's good to see you," she offered.

"Yeah," I said flatly. "It's been a while."

"Yes, I think I last saw you at Marcella's show?"

I snorted in disgust, recoiling at the mere thought of being associated with Marcella's "work." "Yeah, maybe."

After an awkward silence, Emo inquired, "How have you been?"

I stared at her, most likely with my mouth hanging open. *Is she serious?* "I've been better." I snorted.

She nodded and patted Kevin on the bum, motioning for him to sit. "I'm sorry to hear that," she said with more authenticity than I could fathom.

I cleared my throat. "And you?" I asked, fully afraid of the answer.

She stared blankly at me and nodded. "It's been a rough few months, but I'm good. My place reopens next week. I took a little hiatus to grieve. But I have a new show complete and a few artists chomping at the bit. My manager sent out invitations last week. Unfortunately, many will come to gawk at me just to pry, not to see my work or the performing artist of the night."

"Yeah." I cleared my throat again. "I'm sure there will be some spectators if it is your first show since…" I trailed off.

"Since your dad murdered my dad?" She said it flatly, without room for argument. My heart pounded and I willed myself not to start dry-heaving out the lining of my stomach.

Through gritted teeth, I said, "*My dad is not a murderer.*"

"Okay," she said flatly and sarcastically. She gave Kevin's leash a gentle tug, and he stood. "Well, we aren't two kids on a playground arguing over whose dad is stronger. I'll let you get back to your trance. Nice seeing you."

I stood up abruptly, and the park spun. "Wait," I stammered. "I really did see you on accident."

"I believe you." She nodded with a little shrug. "I was just kidding. We were bound to cross paths eventually in a city of nearly eight million people."

I snorted. "What are you doing in the park playing ball?" The question came out clunkily before I could even pretend to manage the words.

Again, she raised her eyebrow. "What do you mean?"

"I don't understand how you can play ball in the park with a dog named Kevin like your whole life didn't end when Leonard was murdered." My voice cracked and tears came without warning.

Emo patted Kevin's bum again, and he obediently sat. "My whole life didn't end. My dad's earthly life ended. And now I must take care of his dog, *Kevin.*"

She said it with a lightness that made me want to throw back and punch her, which hardly seemed appropriate. Instead, I flopped back down onto the park bench, Emo's knees in my face. I looked up at her, the sun illuminating around her angelic hair like a halo. Squinting, I asked in a different way, "How are you okay to play fetch in the park with a dog named Kevin?"

She nodded to the seat next to me, and I slid over. Kevin followed her. She sat down, and he lay on the grass next to the bench.

A sigh escaped her. "Well, I wasn't okay for a long time. Four months?" she questioned no one and then continued, "But Kevin needed to be taken on walks, and my dad needed me to be okay."

I didn't say anything. Folding my arms across my chest, I let my head fall back. She continued. "I am not suggesting you get a dog. But I would say that Kevin kind of forced me to trudge on, find a place to meditate and experience my grief in nature. I started feeling my dad's presence, his encouragement. I guess, I had to act like I was okay until I was. Some days, I still can be a wreck, but most days, I find something that makes me smile. I focus on that."

The start of a snicker must have appeared on my face because Emo's tone became slightly offensive. "What would you suggest?" she asked flatly.

I shook my head in mindless surrender. "I don't know."

She leaned back on the bench, and I tried to decipher her behavior out of the corner of my eye.

And then she spoke, "You have your work, your mom, your nephews, Marcella—"

I cut her off, "Marcella is a joke, she is every reason not to be okay," I said without emotion, recoiling a bit at such a personal exposé on a park bench.

"Yikes," Emo chimed. "That's not the Marcella I know."

"You must not know her well," I added smugly.

Emo nodded, smiling. "Of course, I do. In ways that count for me. She was my KAPPA GAMMA little sis at NYU. She's a brilliant artist. And we run in similar artsy circles. I have watched her work progress over the years. She is interesting and very funny."

"Funny?" I guffawed. "What's funny about her?"

"Well…" Emo shifted in her seat. "I guess if you must explain to someone how funny someone else is, the point is mute. Regardless, I have always enjoyed Marcella's mind."

The statement resolved several things for me about Emo Pruitt. Primarily, I quickly determined she must be an idiot. That is how she can play ball in the park with a dog named Kevin. I felt done talking to her, and I again wished to be teleported to the safekeeping of my flat.

We didn't speak for several minutes. The entirety of the day was nearly laughable. It was as if I had willed Emo into my existence, and now, I wanted her gone. However, since she was being so cordial, so genuinely friendly, I decided to investigate her further.

"Kevin…" I broke the silence. "He's Leonard's dog… The famous show dog?"

Emo smiled, bending and scratching the dog's nose. "The one and only," she said, lowering her voice to a gruff baby talk, "*Sir Caoimhin, you're a good boy, aren't ya?*"

"Why do you call him Kevin?"

"Kevin is the Irish nickname for Caoimhin." She looked back at me. "He's Irish, *an Irish Setter,* get it?"

"Ah. Yeah," I lied. I get nothing about Irish culture or dogs. "What about you? *Emo?* How'd that come about?"

"I'm named after my dad's mom, Esmerelda Imogene. Dad came up with it, *Honey,*" she teased.

It felt like an intrusion to talk about my dad with Emo, which seemed completely backward, but I said anyway, "Yeah, my dad came up with that too. Not nearly as clever."

She gave Kevin a long pat, leaned back again, and inhaled a deep breath. "When are you going to reopen your restaurant?" she boldly inquired.

Emo Pruitt looked like she was really into Pilates or kickboxing, and she was being more than gracious under the circumstances. A few years ago, the woman beat up a guy on the subway who was harassing some tourists. It was in all the papers. So, while I wanted to retort, "*Back up, bitch! You don't know me!*" I instead said somewhat harshly, "I don't know."

Again, we sat in silence. The sky was just beginning to release its summer hold, and I was just dehydrated enough to be brazen. "My dad didn't kill Leonard."

Emo didn't flinch. She stared straight ahead and said, "My dad didn't write that review of your restaurant."

We turned, as if on cue, to face each other. My eyes were dry and tired. Emo's were clear and she spoke with outrageous confidence, "I can't say what I don't know." She stood, tugging on Kevin's leash. "I can't say your father didn't kill my dad. It is all I know for sure right now. But I know my dad. He didn't write that piece about your restaurant."

I felt myself blinking repeatedly and looking up at her with desperate agreement. "Yes!" I yelped and stood. "I mean, it seemed…" I stumbled to explain. "I knew it was so—"

Emo cut me off. "Lame."

"Yes!" I concurred.

"Look, Clara, er, Honey," she continued. "I'm not sleuthing or out to avenge anything. I know my dad, not past tense. *I know him.* He is always with me, and not in some religious, Helter Skelter, hippie way."

I nodded, pretending not to be suspect of her woo-woo hippiness.

She adjusted her backpack. "I have a date. I need to get moving. But you and my dad had a lot in common. He liked you. He respected you as a chef, and he really enjoyed your food and writing." She reached into her pocket and pulled out her cell phone, checked the time, and then slipped it back in.

She looked at me sternly. "Have you read the review? I mean, lately?"

"Yes," I said, convinced I had it memorized.

"Read it again. He didn't write it." Emo inhaled and I noticed her breath seemed shaky now. "I know my dad better now than I did when he was alive."

"What does that mean?"

Emo snorted a little. "I can talk to him in a way I couldn't before. And now, when I have questions, in the quiet, he is honest with me. You can think whatever you would like about that."

I refrained from saying, *I think you are a hippie* and just nodded.

Emo continued, "I never asked him about why your dad killed him."

I inadvertently yelped, "He didn't!"

Emo held up a long-manicured finger and continued, "I don't have the emotional endurance to know any more than I already know about my dad's death." Her voice cracked and Kevin stirred, ready to be done with our chitchatting. Emo gave some imaginary command that only Kevin knew, and he dropped his head shamefully and sat.

"You know, Clara..." Emo spoke with some newfound authority. "I guess I get it. I don't think I could believe my dad would ever hurt another being. But if I were in your place, I would need to know all the details. I would need to know for sure if my dad was a cold-blooded murderer."

Adrenaline coaxed me, and I considered what a playground fight might look like for just a second, but Emo went on.

"Like I said, I feel I know my dad better in death than in life. But honestly, I think I know your dad better than you did in life."

I must have puffed up because Emo held up her finger again.

"Look up from your prep table, Honey."

"*What?*" I couldn't decipher what was even happening. She was speaking in some witchy code, and I was feeling punchy and terrified at the same time.

"You chefs," she snickered. "Prepping in lieu of eating. Never experiencing anything you create for yourself, never stopping to revel in life's magic. That's why my dad didn't want to be in the kitchen anymore. He was missing the good stuff."

I nodded, my silence all that would quench my parched throat.

"Like I said, my dad enjoyed your writing style and food. And I spoke with him after your event. He was happy. He was fine. You should look up, chef. You should *really* read some of my dad's words. He was a poet. You asked me how I am okay to play fetch in the park? Because my dad taught me to live. He wrote words and said beautiful things. And he encouraged me to never create for anyone but myself."

I huffed a little out of some undefined need to be tough, I guess. Emo continued her speech. "It's good advice. Especially for a chef and food writer."

"Why's that?" I asked.

"You create everything to feed someone else both in word and food. What do you love? What do you want to see?"

"I don't know anymore," I whispered.

"Well...," Emo added. "Maybe when you do, you will find what you are looking for. Aside from that, I'm not sure that I can offer you much more. But, if I can, and it helps you find peace, I am happy to do what I can. You can track me down, *obviously*." She winked and gave a quick tug on Kevin's lead, and he stood.

"Okay," I said. "I, uh, well, thank you. I will read it again."

"All right then, off to get a pretty. I have a new guy to lead around by the nose. Nice running into you."

I watched Emo and Kevin leave the park. Every inch of my body ached, and I couldn't imagine getting home; however, with my phone dead and my desperate need to read that article, I tugged at my souvenir t-shirt and hiked my way to the nearest cab.

At home, I dumped a bottle of wine in a tumbler, downed it in unreasonable, compulsory gulps, and then opened another bottle, imagining the fermented grape juice washing my pain away. I grabbed my stash of Xanax from my purse and swallowed two. I had to move quickly before the meds lulled me into the welcomed embrace of a chemically induced coma. But I decided to pretend I was not a full-blown alcoholic/prescription-drug addict and grabbed a wine glass off the shelf and filled the glass. I flopped on the couch with my laptop, opened it, and typed in the necessary information.

The page loaded and my stomach rocked and rolled as alcohol and barbiturates threatened to do as they promised and take me under.

Honey's is Disappointing: Don't Bother
Leonard Pruitt

Unfortunately, I had dinner at Chef Clara Honeycutt's new 57th location of the legendary Honey's on Friday night. While Chef "Honey" usually has been called a good cook for her Southern Cuisine and French style, she has gotten cocky, careless, or just never had any talent to begin with. The courses were rushed, the service was pathetic, and I spent the night in the bathroom praying to the porcelain gods. I suspect the limp cilantro had traces of salmonella. But I guess we will find out when the rest of the evening's patrons confess, they were up all night, Chef Honey's delicacies spewing out both ends. In short, Clara Honeycutt is a hack, with no vision for elegance and a nasty kitchen. Honey's is POISON.

If I must give a star, here's ONE for the clean water glass.

I shook my head, confusion nipping at me, my stomach angry, my head soggy with too much information—a result of confusion from not enough and too much wine. I had rehashed my encounters with Pruitt over and over. The night of the event, I visited his table between three of the courses. He gushed over everything. I had seen him in the bar area talking to my mother. When he walked away, Mother smiled brightly and gave me two thumbs up. Pruitt was one critic I knew loved my food. Heck, he even liked me. We had met at a few events. On one occasion, he told me that he subscribed to *The Fork* just to read my column. But there was something else that bothered me now. Emo was right. The wording of Pruitt's review, the article was just so… *lame*. Writing about food was something Pruitt and I had talked about at a food writers' conference a few years ago. And Pruitt and I agreed, writing about food was often harder than creating the food. So many senses are involved in the culinary experience. It takes a wordsmith who understands the complexities of dining to write articles that can somewhat compare.

I clicked on another link title: "The Criminal Behaviors of Chef Colby Chantal". I drank from my wine glass as the bitter brew melted and mixed with drugs. I yawned and stretched, continuing to read, awestruck by Leonard's astonishingly powerful command of critique.

IN LIEU OF EATING

Oh, chef, how is it possible that I could find your bouillabaisse so repugnant? Your prawns mealy, your salad, a wilted disaster that could've been easily mistaken for a cheese course. The rest of the courses were juvenile in creation, and yet, masterful in plate presentation. It is this charm, paired with the warmth of your establishment, that temporarily lulled me into the belief, this is where I will eat from now on. It is a nod to the complexities Chantal seeks in his kitchen and the diligence he demands in the dining room. The food, maybe three stars, but the environment, service, and chef's involvement in the experience are just seductive enough, I ordered a third entrée in hopes of proving myself wrong. Alas, the food is average at best...

I scrolled and willed my eyes to read more. Leonard Pruitt was dynamic and passionate. One article I found was over two thousand words. But he was prolific and specific about his reasons. He used descriptions such as exquisite, dumpster fire, a rude awakening, inventive, and tastes like kipper snacks. So, what happened that made Pruitt turn on me? And why had he done it in such a soggy oatmeal kind of way?

Unless Emo was right, and he didn't turn on me. But if he didn't write it, who did? And what did it have to do with my dad?

I read and dozed, clicking on link after link, and just before the wine and pills demanded my full attention, I read the last piece of an article Leonard had written on September 19, 2001, eight days after the World Trade Center violence. My eyes struggled to finish.

Will this be read? An opinion piece by a South-African immigrant, single father, with a dying, dementia-ravaged mother, working as a food critic in a city that never sleeps? A city that never sleeps should not know of such nightmares. And yet, surely this cannot be real? My parents fled their country because of violence. But I don't think any human can fathom what violence looks like until we meet with it ourselves. And then, it is every bit as horrific as we might have imagined.

Violence is an aggressive and selfish energy. It rudely interrupts the energy of peace with its demand to be served, to meet with what it wants. But from my office, as the smoke and smog still bellow up from the tragedy of a now-distant morning, I know violence by a new name, hate.

What else but hate has the aggressive, selfish energy that would snuff out life with such cruelty?

The last sentence stabbed at my alcohol-soaked gut. I dropped my wine empty glass and listened as it bounced and rolled on the hardwood beneath me. Slamming my laptop shut, I tossed it into my stylish, grass-green chair. I pulled a fleece blanket off the back of the sofa, curled into a ball, and cried myself to sleep. I barely admonished myself for not charging my phone as I mentally reminded myself, tomorrow I will meet with Lance Vega. He will help me. I know he will.

And I passed out, in lieu of consciousness.

Appetizer

The next morning, I found myself with a little pep in my step, despite my self-inflicted Xanax-wine-sleep stupor. Today, I had an appointment with Lance Vega, co-founder of the justice organization Free Me. The organization was launched by Lance's mother and father, Lolly and Martin Vega, after Lance, their only child, was wrongly convicted of the rape and murder of a neighborhood girl. Martin Vega happened to be an old acquaintance of my dad's. My mother and dad made monetary contributions to Free Me, and one or both of my parents served on the board at various times. I did recall hearing that Martin had passed away a few years ago—I think he had fought cancer in his later years—but as I googled and researched ways to help Dad, Martin and Lolly Vega both sprung to my mind. It was only when reading an online article that I remembered that Mother and Dad had attended Martin's funeral.

It felt as if I was out of the loop on everything that used to matter. But today's meeting with Lance would be the first truly proactive effort I could make in spearheading my dad's vindication. I pulled on gray linen slacks, shocked at the loose fit, but certain, once my appetite returned, I would be back in the land of fourteen plus-plus. What some might call a size sixteen.

I tied my hair in a loose bun and picked a yellow, billowy, soft, button-down blouse, slipped on sandal flats, and rushed to meet Axel. I was surprised to see Axel standing next to the sedan, with the back door opened for me, like a chauffeur.

"Morning, Axel." I speed-walked around him and his odd chivalry. "Seriously? I will just sit in the front."

Axel pushed the back door shut, climbed inside, slammed the door belligerently, and threw his flat driver's hat at me.

"Hey!" I barked. "What was that?"

Axel grunted, "Nothing." He pulled away from the curb, looking over his shoulder.

Our eyes met, and I batted my freshly styled lashes. "What's the matter?" I cooed at him.

"Nothing," he spat flatly.

We rode in silence for several blocks en route downtown to the Free Me offices.

Axel didn't ask how I was doing or if I had heard any news about Dad. The tension, thick like stale, day-old cornbread, made me feel even more anxious about the meeting with Lance. I decided to break the ice.

"Lady troubles?" I finally poked him in the ribs.

He grunted with a tone of abhorrence. "If those ladies are named Honeycutt, yeah."

I let out a groan of disgust. "Great. What did Marcella do now?"

Axel snorted. A contemptuous grin exposed a deep, familiar dimple in his dark-complexioned cheek. "You are a piece of work, Clara." He spat out the words with his eyes intent on traffic.

I gawked at him with confused anxiousness. *Clara?* This wasn't about my sister; this was about *me*. I looked out the window, searching my mind for the vast gap in our common car-ride banter. Finally, in no mood for more drama, I turned to face him.

"What is your problem?" I semi-begged.

"Oh, I don't know." He scratched his neatly manicured, stubbly chin. "I guess, when I asked you to meet me for dinner last night with my cousin, Diego, and his wife, who were only in town for one night…"

"Oh, my god, Axel!" I squealed like a child. "I am so sorry. I can't even begin—"

"Then just don't." He said it flatly with more than a twinge of scorn and shrugged.

Having been employed for ten years by our family, I knew Axel well enough not to carry on when he or myself called it quits during our conversation. I uncharacteristically wanted to gush and beg. But there was no point when I had so blatantly screwed up. He pulled the car up in front of the Free Me complex and threw it into park.

"Get out," he said.

"I am so sorry, Axel. My head… I mean, I just… Raven had…" I had a litany of excuses, none of them worthy of repeating. "I am sorry I forgot about dinner with your cousin."

Axel nodded. "I gotta go get your mother and take her to the podiatrist. Text me when you're done. I'll try and get back quick."

"Don't worry about…" I touched his hand, and he quickly pulled it away, shocking me with his callousness.

"Axel!" I yelped. "I made a mistake! I need you to say it's okay!" My plea came out in an unreasonable squeal, and mentally, I admonished myself for being a girl.

"It's *not* okay, Clara." He shook his head. "I didn't want to have to tell Diego all the gory details or anything else about this whole mess with your dad! And guess what?" He threw his hands up, his eyes wild with betrayal.

APPETIZER

Axel needed me, and I didn't show up.

He dropped his hands onto the steering wheel and spoke again, this time monitoring the volume of his valid complaints. "That was the conversation all damn night. Diego will go back to Argentina and tell my mother, and she is going to freak out. *Now*, I am going to have to go there! None of this would be a problem if you had been there! They wouldn't have asked…" He trailed off.

I nodded, knowing that Axel's family had been terribly distraught when he moved to New York. Even after Axel's mother and sister came to see him, staying in the carriage house with him, they had passionately yearned for him to return home with them. Every Sunday, for the last ten years, Axel's mother would call weeping, pleading with him to return to her. Now, I had really screwed things up for him. Diego had a tragedy to report to Axel's family about our family. Oh, and it involved a brutal murder.

I checked my watch and clamored to exit the car while our friendship was still intact.

"I am *really* sorry, Axel." I threw my purse over my shoulder. "Can we talk after this meeting?"

"I guess I have no choice since you'll be in the car."

"Sorry," I said once more for good measure. I shut the door and went to meet with the only person I knew of who could help me free my dad, *Lance Vega*.

Thirty-six years after my father christened me his *Honey*, and at least twenty-six years since the nickname should have been archived, I had opted to keep it, sugary-sweet though it be—a moniker that clashes with nearly every part of my person, yet it was consistent for one tactical reason.

Power.

The name *Honey* puts prey at ease, and it serves as a great disguise—a misdirection to those who do not know me well. Then, to those convinced I must be as warm and gooey as such a name might suggest, I can catch them unaware, squashing a soul into dust with one look if the need arises—then leveling up my game with a whisper of insult and injury just under my fiery breath. And *I always win,* whether I am right or not. After my "last word," I go silent. My unwitting opponent then volleys their offense or defense with *"But Honey… !"*

Once the retaliatory bomb has been detonated, I move in with more of my end-game goal: me being right. I was determined to make today no different.

I entered the office lobby, bright with brassy fixtures and sensible, green-and-navy plaid, high-traffic carpet. But the once-welcomed smell of freshly brewed coffee nearly chased me from the building.

I steadied my resolve. The lobby of the Free Me office was decorated in heavy, lawyer-esque furniture, with marble end tables and smart, serious lamps. I felt small, out of place. Odd. I never feel small and out of place. A gag rose in my throat, and my stomach gurgled rather loudly as I stepped toward the receptionist. The enormous Free Me logo stood with pride above the receptionist's desk, an emblem of rogue justice. The morning sun prioritized the gold-embossed insignia, radiating its legacy of victory in a reflective light show of hope-filled beams and rays.

"Good morning. May I help you?" A trim, older woman looked over her glasses at me as she rose to greet me from behind her enormous, lacquered, cherry-wood desk.

"Yes. Hello. I am Honey—*Clara,*" I corrected. "Clara Honeycutt."

"Yes, Miss Honeycutt, Mr. Vega is expecting you. Can I get you a cup of—?"

"No!" I deflected with such exaggerated opposition, one might believe the woman was about to finish the sentence with "arsenic?" I scrambled to recover my genteel upbringing. "I mean, no. Thank you, though. I am fine."

She nodded. "Very well. If you change your mind, my name is Debby. Just let me know if you need anything."

I bit my tongue so as not to pipe, "Debby, I need only to free my father!" But I opted to save my pleas for Lance. I sat with deliberate calm on a luscious, fine-burgundy leather sofa. Moments later, I heard a buzz, and Debby alerted me, "Ms. Honeycutt, Mr. Vega will see you now."

I forgot my decent upbringing entirely at that point and skipped-ran-sprinted to Lance's office.

"Hey!" Lance greeted me with a bear hug like we were long-lost family.

"Hey," I returned, narrowly managing to keep myself poised, and then I... *burst into tears.*

"Oh!" He guided me to a high-back, regal-looking chair. "Sit, sit. Let me get you a glass of water."

I grabbed his wrist, looking up at him with the desperation of a naked person in need of cover. "No." My voice cracked with want. "No, please, Lance. I need..." He knew what I needed: my father free. "I need to say... *all of it.* I must explain."

Lance moved to the chair opposite me and turned it. When he sat, our knees touched. He laid his strong, brown hand on my shoulder. "Tell me, Clara. Tell me what you know, what you suspect. Everything."

It took me all of five seconds—actually, it was more like an hour—to unleash. It was a culmination of frustration and confusion, but Lance didn't ask any questions. When I was finished, mascara running down my cheeks and a steady stream of snot pouring off my nose, Lance stood.

Through bleary eyes, I watched his tall, slender frame move to a closet. He pulled a new box of Kleenex out and returned to his post across from me. He opened the box, offered me one, and said, "Okay.

Now, I know the emotion and the terror of all this, but Honey..." Lance snorted a laugh. "Well, that is disarming. I don't normally call anyone *Honey*." He shook his head as if to regroup. "Honey, I need you to take a deep breath." I followed his lead, raggedly sucking oxygen between sobs and hiccup-laced whimpers.

"Now...," Lance comforted. "I need some facts."

I yelped, "Those are the facts! Thursday was the surprise party. Friday was the soft opening for an exclusive list. Saturday was the grand opening. Leonard Pruitt was invited by *my father* to the grand opening event. Nothing, I mean, *nothing*, went poorly. In fact, Pruitt told me to look for his 'rave review' in the next few days. I slept through Sunday and Monday. Tuesday, Leonard's review came out. Thursday, his body was found, and my dad turned himself in. But Lance... it doesn't make sense. I was shocked by the negative report, having not a single concern. Pruitt had dined on *all* the featured menu items. And he ordered two slices of my famous lemon-blueberry cake."

Lance's appetite interrupted, "That is my favorite! You know that cake is what we have—"

I interrupted, "Yes. I know." Not wanting to be rude but resigned to stay on track, I pressed on. "I know your mother orders my cakes all the time for celebrations. But Lance, I haven't marinated, sautéed, roasted, grilled, licked a spoon, or cooled a layer since Pruitt's article exposed me as a 'hack, with no vision for elegance and a nasty kitchen.'"

Lance nodded. "And I know that is not true of you. However, that article... That is the ace in the hole for the district attorney. Should your father recant his confession, that would be the metaphorical smoking gun for a trial."

"But..." The yelp escaped me. "*It isn't! My dad hardly reacted!*" I inhaled, intentionally lowering my intensity. "Dad soothed me, promising that one lousy write-up among the *thousands* of excellent reviews would not impact us or the restaurant."

Lance raised a dark eyebrow, shooting me a curious look. "Wait? Your father wasn't mad about Pruitt's critique?"

"No!" I pleaded, reaching for another tissue. I blew my nose and continued, "That is what I do not understand. Before Pruitt's body was found, two more reports came out chastising Pruitt's evaluation, questioning Pruitt's credibility, not mine." I sniffled. "Lance, my dad was not upset or bothered. He was rock-solid." I deepened my voice to mimic my dad's tone as I quoted him verbatim: *'There is nothing to even discuss, no need to retaliate. Honey's reputation in the arena of Manhattan's fine dining far exceeds the exaggerated opinions and nonsensical drivel of one dreary food critic.'*"

Lance leaned back in the chair and rubbed his chin. "Honey," he began, "I hear you. I really do. I won't say that I understand exactly how you feel. But I do understand this case is not as cut and dry as it appears in the media. However, the lawyer in me must remind you, your father confessed."

"I don't understand..."

Lance held up a hand, stopping me. "Honey..." He leaned in, placing one hand on my knee. "I understand, but there is not much I can do with a confession on the record—"

I interrupted, "But that's the—"

"A confession your dad will not recant," Lance finished. He leaned back in his chair, casually crossed his arms, and began again. "My mother visited your father after he confessed. He was being held at Rikers."

I shook my head in denial. "I didn't know. He won't talk to me about the case."

"Well," he sighed. "Mom and I have both seen him."

I perked up. "*What?* You've seen him?"

"Yeah. Like I said, my mom went before Tom was moved to Attica. She offered our services, imploring him to let us help him." Lance shook his head. "His words to her were the exact same ones he said to me: '*I did it. There is no reason for you to concern yourself further.*'"

"When did you see him?" I begged.

"After you emailed me, I sent him a letter." Lance reached his long arm over to the desk, picked up a file, leafed through it, and then plucked out a letter, which he handed to me. "See? I offered to represent him. I invited him to add me to his legal counsel visitor roster."

"So, you are representing him?" The question exploded from me in a wave of nearly cautious optimism. I shakily handed him the letter back.

"Nope," Lance answered flatly. "Honestly, if I was, I wouldn't be able to discuss this with you. I was, however, notified that he would meet with me. But he didn't fill out any of the documents and would not agree to partner with me for a reversal."

"Why?" I begged.

Lance shrugged. "We met in the common visitor area. He was adamant, he beat and killed Pruitt and dumped his body. Then he said not to contact him again." He leaned forward. "Honey, he said to tell you, he is sorry. He lost his temper. He wants you to treat this, his life sentence, *to accept it,* as you would his death." He grabbed my hand.

It lay limp beneath his grasp as my disbelief competed with... something. Resolve? No, not that. I cannot bring resolution to something that has none.

"*Lost his temper?*" I whimpered.

"Tom's words *exactly*. '*I lost my temper.*'"

I dropped my face in my hands, closing my eyes tightly. *Rewind, rewind, rewind,* I chanted in my mind. I just want to play back this horror, this unbelievable, impossible monster *that was just not possible*. I steadied myself, determined to exhaust every single inconsistency, desperate to convince Lance, *There is no way my dad could do this*.

"Dad doesn't lose his temper." I said it flatly.

"Well, he says he did," Lance countered.

I stood up and began to pace the office, feeling like a caged animal. Frustration and impotence nipped at me. I stopped in front of the enormous window facing a green space in a tidy courtyard. Wrapping my arms around myself, I choked as I spoke. "Who loses their temper, beats someone beyond recognition, and shoots them point-blank in the face?" I swung around my arms and then started flailing them. "Tell me, Lance? Who does something so vile? Horrific? *Risking everything*. Then dumps the body in the Hudson? Who does that and then says, 'Oops, yeah, gosh, sorry, I lost my temper.'"

Lance stood and sauntered toward me, taking my shoulders in his hands. "I agree. But he won't talk to me. And—"

"*One Cobalt Blue Shot of Tequila!*" I interrupted.

"What?" Lance stepped back to investigate my enthusiasm.

I pulled his arm, guiding us back to the chairs. We sat, me on the edge of my seat, where I steadied my overzealous tone. "That's how patient and loving Dad is. My sister, Marcella, did a one-woman show, and the title was *One Cobalt Blue Shot of Tequila*. She rallied Dad to produce it. And Marcella doesn't borrow a few bucks and rig some stage lights. She hired a marketing team, a publicist, and a director. She even tried to rent out the Met." I shook my head, eternally incredulous that I am somehow related to Marcella.

"Dear lord, how can I still live on this small island? Bottom line is, the one-night show's final price tag was about $700,000. Which the press found out, and the whole thing became a mess. The entire time, I was thinking, I am going to have to move to Utah, and my mom and dad are in freaking *la-la* land, *encouraging her!*" I calmed myself. "Sorry, my sister and I have… Well… I hate her. But the show?" I dramatically semi-preformed from my seat. "Lights dim, curtain goes up, spotlight center stage, *Marcella Monet*. She is full-on buck-naked but for a wooden clothespin on each of her nipples and an empty can of Pepsi glued to her crotch. Also, she is wearing one pink cowboy boot and one orange flip-flop." Lance's eyes were wide and his mouth slightly open. I continued.

"There's rainforest sounds playing over the sound system, and then a man in a gorilla suit comes out pushing a jukebox. He pushes a button on the music machine, and this '50s song starts playing. And that is when Marcella says, '*I'll have one cobalt blue shot of tequila!*' And the gorilla swings back a hairy arm and slaps Marcella. *Like, really smacks her.* She collapsed to the floor, fully mooning the audience, further confirming to 1,100 ticket holders, Marcella is not a natural blonde."

Lance blushed and shifted awkwardly in his seat.

I continued, "And the curtain closes. The whole place goes dark, and then native drumming starts, *boom, boom, boom*. The curtain opens and Marcella is back, stage left, spotlight on her. Now she is wearing an English riding suit, boots, helmet, and whip. And then a white horse walks on stage right with LOOK AT WHAT WE'VE DONE NYC spray painted on its body in red. And Marcella clicks her heels three times and barks in short, quick words, 'One…cobalt…blue…shot…of… tequila!' And, as if by some cosmos magic, the horse shits on stage." I dramatically add, "*Curtain closes.*" Finally, I take a deep bow in my seat. Flopping back in the chair, as if too fatigued by the performance to stand, I add, "The horse shit wasn't part of the show, but the art world wet itself." Lance still bore astonishment on his face, and I wasn't even finished. "Now, a lot of people hated it, but there are people walking free in the city, behaving as normal, everyday citizens, who actually said things like, '*incredibly wise and breathtaking.*' '*Brave, bold, and electrifying!*' And my favorite, '*Finally, an artist who really understands the weight of racism on our culture.*'"

Lance held up a finger to stop me. "I don't understand how you feel this exonerates your father."

"He didn't kill her. Dad brought Marcella flowers and said with open arms, 'My baby!' And he meant it. She screamed like a psychopath, '*Please get out! It was a disaster!*' And then my mom went looking for someone notable to coax Marcella into the afterparty with Tom Cruise or Gloria Estefan."

"They were there? "Lance asked, starstruck.

"*Everybody* was there," I continued. "Money makes people stupid. People will put on a tux and flashy, impractical shoes and then spend an evening with horse shit on stage and call it art if it means they were seen. But love makes you stupid-er. My dad didn't kill Marcella. I wanted to kill her. I want to kill *me* for telling you the story and then come back from the dead and kill you because you shouldn't have to know about that level of crazy."

We both belly-laughed, which triggered sobbing for me, of course. Lance offered another tissue.

"Tom Honeycutt doesn't lose his temper," I pleaded on, wiping at my cheeks and then under my dripping faucet of a nose. "Dad isn't frantic. He isn't panicked. He sees no evil! *God!*" I howled. "What is he seeing? Oh, my heart. I can't… *This is not possible.* I need someone to help me help him!" I begged and sobbed some more.

After several moments, with my body still shuddering, we sat in the quiet, and Lance rubbed his face. "Honey." He cleared his throat. "Tom won't talk to us. He won't sign the releases. And you need to know, *I know* how you feel. Hopeless and helpless." His voice cracked. "And *imprisoned* by the situation, but I don't have the manpower, not even if

IN LIEU OF EATING

I pulled attorneys in from other states, to help. I don't have the hours necessary to help someone that does not want help." Lance cleared his throat. "*And* I need to tell you…" He picked up another piece of paper and handed it to me. "Honey, uh, *Clara*, I mean, I am sorry. It's hard to have this conversation and start with *Honey*."

"Disarming, huh?" I snorted, wiping my nose again. "I can alpha dog anyone if they must fight back with '*But Honey!*'"

Lance smiled, nodding. So, I continued to plead my case.

"Okay, *Mr. Vega*. My dad doesn't want your help. But as you said, *I am imprisoned*. Unjustly. I can hire you. Or donate. But just think of it like this: Why would Tom Honeycutt be so quick to rebuke help if he didn't have something to hide?"

Lance nodded. "Well, the DA would argue the opposite, that Tom did kill Pruitt, and now, he can't face his family. Shame is a dead ringer for a guy like your dad. The argument could be made that he snapped and killed Pruitt and is taking his medicine for the crime."

"Don't say that!" I yelped it like a child.

Lance sighed, rubbing his face. "Okay." He leaned back, staring into space, and then finally spoke. Lance pursed his lips, empathy oozing, yet he appeared increasingly troubled; I quickly realized he was pitying me.

"Do you know of anyone that would want your dad out of the way?"

"Just my evil sister. I can see Marcella pulling a Menendez Brothers kind of thing."

"Are you serious? She was out of the country. Marcella was at a polo match in London. She left the morning after your grand opening," Lance countered.

I snorted. "Oh, my god! You don't believe that she was seriously invited by *the queen*, do you? Marcella crashed that polo match because the guy that dumped her is the son of an ambassador, or some nonsense. She put those pictures all over Facebook—"

Lance cut me off. "Exactly. She didn't do it."

"She could have hired it done," I argued.

"Honey?"

"Yes, dear?" I purred, hoping I might still be able to somehow charm Lance into investigating just a little more.

Lance looked at me sternly. "You need to be serious."

"I'm sorry. It's just really hard. I really hate her. I wish Marcella did do it."

We simultaneously guffawed—until I once again burst into tears.

This time, Lance gushed a little. Compassionately, he purred, "Clara, Tom is going to be okay. You are going to be okay. You must decide to be okay. Believe it. See it. *Feel it.*"

The wind spurted from my lungs in hyper-disappointment. Because suddenly, I knew.

Lance wasn't going to help me. Lance believed my dad killed Leonard Pruitt. I wasn't alone in the room, but I felt every bit of my isolation.

Snot was pouring off my face in a river now. I heaved out a sob. "So…" I inhaled a jagged breath. "You can't help me?"

Lance moved to the big window. He stood with his hands on his narrow hips and said nothing for a long time. I held my breath, desperate for him to turn to face me, a huge grin on his face, declaring a *Eureka!* moment that would end this horror. But he didn't. I watched as Lance's hands slipped from his hips to rest in his pricey suit pant pockets. His shoulders relaxed, and he moved to his desk and sat. As if in slow motion, he moved some papers on his desk, folded his hands, looked me straight in the eyes, and said, "No." He lowered his head. "But it isn't because I don't want to help you."

"Then why?"

He slid back in the luxurious leather chair and exhaled. "I have nothing to work with, Honey."

"But—!"

Lance held up his hand. "If we had something to go on, maybe. But we don't. And, most importantly, Tom doesn't want my help. And your dad *really* wants you to let this go."

Lance spun his chair, picked up a piece of paper off the desk, and then handed it to me.

"What's this?"

"A formal correspondence from Attica."

I tried to read through blurry eyes. "Removal from visitors list?"

"Keep reading," Lance prodded.

"Lance Vega, Lolly Vega, Rose Merchant…" I stopped. *"Rose is our family attorney!* Why would he do that?" I continued to read. "Clara…" The entire office spun around me. "Wait? *What?* What is this?"

Lance leaned his elbows on his desk and lifted his shoulders in a shrug. "He's removing you from his visitors list, plain and simple."

I shot up out of the chair. "Plain and simple?!"

Lance motioned for me to sit, but I rebelliously ignored him. "He doesn't want this line of questioning, Honey. He doesn't want you going down this path. Now I don't know him well, or you. But I do know, there must be a reason he confessed and a reason he doesn't want my help." He paused. "Or yours."

My heart was racing; the entire debacle continued to make less and less sense.

"The review!" I bounced toward Lance. "I do have something!"

Lance folded his arms. "Honey, we've already been—"

"No! Lance, listen…" I decided to trim my enthusiasm, so I forced contemplative, cognitive control. "Leonard didn't write that review."

"What are you talking about?" Lance's eyebrows raised with peaked curiosity.

"I mean," I sputtered, but I wanted to be coherent. I straightened my back, raised my chin, and spoke. "I am a professional chef, but I'm also a professional writer. Or, well, I was. I am pretty sure I was fired for… It doesn't matter!" I gushed on, "Leonard and I knew each other. He liked my writing style. But I swear to you, he was the reason I was able to write. Leonard's writing is delicious. It is intoxicating. Leonard wrote with passion, humor, and honesty. And I really did grow as a writer because he was such an amazing wordsmith." I stopped just shy of saying, *And I wanted to be better than him because I have to be the best.*

"Pardon the lawyer in me," Lance interrupted. "Maybe that was all Pruitt honestly had to say about your food?"

"Nope." I shook my head in rapid defiance. "No. That is not what happened, Lance. I talked to Leonard that night. He spoke to my mother. And I can't be sure, but the Leonard Pruitt I know would have told me if there was a problem. He wouldn't do that for everyone. But Lance, I saw him." Tears escaped me again, and I felt the fury rise, though not at Lance. I was furious with myself for being so desperate and weepy.

At that moment. there was a brisk knock at the door, and this stupid-happy woman came bouncing in and squeaked, "*Lance Martin Vega!* Did you make this woman cry?"

Lance stood and handed me the whole box of Kleenex this time. "Saraphina, this is Clara Honeycutt."

I stuck out a snotty hand and answered, "Please, call me Honey."

Saraphina squealed decibels above what can be heard by humans. Dogs were howling in response. "*Oooh!* If I get to call you *Honey*, you can call me *Sara!*"

Luckily, because if this woman got any happier, I was going to kick her in her teeth, my phone chimed. I slid it out of my pocket and checked the text.

Mom: *BO11*

Which was our 911 for my nephew, Bo, terrorizing the family with misdemeanor criminal activities and a less than passionate commitment to high school. With that legitimate excuse, I hurried, "It's a pleasure. Hey, I gotta go, Lance. Mom needs me."

"No problem," he said as he followed me to the door. "I have meetings the rest of the day. But this evening, I will do some reading. It was good to see you, Honey."

"It was good to see you too, Lance." I looked up at him with the biggest, roundest puppy dog eyes I could muster. Our eyes locked, and he nodded.

And for just a moment, I took a deep breath of relief, in lieu of anguish.

Salad

On a bench under the trees outside the Free Me office, I called my mother and then Bo's school. Bo got caught cheating on his chemistry test. While on the phone with the school's administrator, I once again fell apart. *Maybe I should ditch mascara once and for all*, I thought. The administrator, taken aback by my unusual weepy behavior, ended the conversation with, "How about we just let this one slide?"

I grappled with my terrible *parenting* skills and then talked myself off the ledge...*because I am not a parent.*

I sent Axel a text, letting him know I was finished with my meeting. He immediately responded, *Find a cafe and eat something decent. I will be well after one o'clock getting back.* Irritated but restless, I spun in a quick circle, assessing my location. I texted him back: *fine.*

Axel answered *K*. My least favorite text response. Just type *Okay*. Is tapping out an "O" with your thumb too much to ask for? I hitched my bag over my shoulder and walked to Chester's Pub, where I knew it wouldn't smell like coffee; plus, it was the only pub within walking distance open before lunch. Chester's also had a sad little internet cafe. I was hopeful I could hop on a computer and do some digging.

When I opened the wood-framed glass door, and a gush of ice-cold "paid-for" air assaulted me, I sighed in welcomed relief. The little Irish man behind the bar bellowed, "What'll you have, missy?"

"A Bloody Mary?" I questioned, wondering if the Irish know about celery salt.

"Aye," he answered. "Sit wherever."

"Actually…" I pointed to the back of the bar. "…can I use one of your computers?"

"Yeah, sure." He nodded. "Password is GUINNESS. All caps."

I nodded, refraining from commenting, "Of course, it is." I made my way to a pre-Y2k device that wanted to be a computer but was coming in at a close second to a very big calculator. I admonished myself for leaving my laptop at home but clicked out *GUINNESS* on the bulky keys and watched the little wheel whirl as it attempted to connect.

"Here you go, miss." The barkeep set a large, un-frosted mug onto a tattered cork coaster. The celery looked limp, and celery seeds skimmed the top of a sad slice of lime.

"Thanks," I said, smiling politely.

"Anything else?" he prodded. "I can whip you up some toast and hash. You don't want to be drinking on an empty stomach this early in the day."

"Oh." I chewed on my lip, afraid of this man's hash, and more interested in some research and booze. But then I relented, unable to recall the last bite of food I had eaten. "Sure. But can I just have some toast?"

"Yeah, sure." He headed off, leaving me to my search.

I logged into my email to send Lance a quick "thank you and don't forget to read more" note. Begrudgingly, I was forced to click on an email from my editor at *The Fork*. I read,

Clara, if you are no longer wanting to write for The Fork, *I understand. We were able to cover for you in the months after your family's upheaval. But I am going to need something from you within the week, or I will need to move forward with a new contributor.*

Honey, I just need to know what you want to do. I am happy to cover for you for a while longer, but—please. It would be helpful to know what your plans are. Best —Jane

I can't say I didn't see that coming. But, for now, it was the least of my concerns.

I typed *Leonard Pruitt* into the search bar and was met with the same findings I had been accustomed to, nauseating sorrow with a side of bewilderment. Despite that, I needed to go through the information again. But this time, I wasn't just mindlessly pouring over opinion and clickbait drivel. I wanted to see more of Leonard's work and prove he didn't write the review. Although, I had no idea what that proof would help prove.

I clicked on the obituary, and the toast arrived as the page loaded at a snail's pace. I forced a bite of the parched, dry bread as the bartender stood over me, eagerly awaiting my approval. I choked and chewed and gave him a thumbs up.

"Good! Good! Can I get you anything else?"

I held up my empty mug. "Yeah." I swallowed. "Another Bloody Mary. Make it a double."

He nodded and left me to scroll.

The page slowly opened, and Leonard Pruitt's wide smile appeared. He was stunning in a short, faded afro, completely gray, and a neatly manicured, full beard that was snow-white, with well-defined, dark, silver curls. His skin, a creamy, dark-chocolate brown, made his teeth appear blindingly white. But his eyes…the most interesting hazel shade with swirls of copper and gold. Much like the gold leaf I used to top my decadent Gold Digger Napoleon pastries at the restaurant.

IN LIEU OF EATING

Tears burned my eyes, just as they always do when I acknowledge Pruitt as the human I knew. I clicked away and followed the link to the article that Pruitt wrote about my restaurant.

"Can I get you anything?" A short, wide, redheaded woman now stood over me, her greasy apron way too close to my face. "Maybe ya should have yourself some coffee?" Her accent was thick with a Celtic drawl.

"Um…," I stumbled, really wanting another Bloody Mary but thinking this brute of a woman was going to cut me off. "May I have a coke with ice?"

This somehow pleased the matron, and she nodded. "Sure, but I only got Pepsi in the can. I can pour it over ice fer ya."

"That will be fine, thank you." I nodded and continued to read.

The barmaid distracted me again. "Lass, I got some stew in the back. How 'bout a bowl?"

I nodded. "Yes. Thank you. And a glass of something red, please. House, whatever you recommend."

She eyed me over her glasses with a "tsk, tsk" stare, but I ignored her. I would also probably ignore the stew, but I was on a roll and just wanted more alcohol and solace. I continued to click and scroll, seeing the same consistencies, along with Leonard's passion and dynamism, only further leaving me certain, something else had to have happened. My thoughts thumped and whirled until they regurgitated the same sickening question: *Who wrote that review?*

My stew was delivered with a glass of burgundy. The soup was gray, with a single sliver of orange carrot clinging to the side of the bowl, a stranger in an Irish pot. I barely choked down one bite and then neglected the rest for the wine. I clicked on a link, Of Summer and Sandwiches, and waited for the page to load.

The piece was more personal. Pruitt spoke in romantic metaphors, turning out descriptive, personal tales of his favorite picnic spots, ones he frequented with his daughter or a "lady friend" he did not name. My throat tightened. The humanity of Leonard… The depths of loss wrapped bony fingers around my windpipe.

I was jerked from my scourged imaginings when my phone pinged out an alert. I picked it up, logged off the dinosaur computer, paid my check, and rushed to meet Axel out front.

It was 1:15 when I finally climbed into the car. Axel didn't get out of the car or open my door. He didn't ask how the meeting went or if there was any good news about Dad. Finally, I asked, "How long are you going to punish me?"

Axel shook his head. Extending out a long breath, he finally answered, "I am not punishing you. Punishment is a means of forcing someone to do something to conform them to your own desires. You are just facing the consequences of your actions."

I snorted, affronted by his tone. "All right then, *professor*, what are my consequences? Just tell me so we can be friends again." Then, to ease up on my snark, I playfully jiggled my body like a child. "I want to tell you what I learned from Lance! Hurry up! Let's be friends."

Axel was quiet, creeping the long black sedan through the traffic. I kept my eyes on him, confused by his vibe. Finally, he sighed and said, "I am not responsible for your consequences. I am responsible for mine. You are not a good friend, Clara. I befriended you," Axel scoffed. "I have admired you, I think. No, I know, I loved you. I've always considered the possibility of something more—more than what we've had. But you are not a good friend. I must deal with my illusion of friendship or hope of real romance. I must heal from that hurt. That is my consequence."

I had no words. Although Axel's statements—the confession and verdict—seemed better suited for a line of poetic yet tragic greeting cards. My throat was hot, my mouth void of any moisture.

Shockingly, I didn't cry. I just stared at him. He pulled the car into the garage. Which caught me further by surprise. Axel always drops the family off at the front of the house. He shut off the car and turned to face me. The dim lights of the garage security light barely illuminated his dark features.

Again, he spoke, "I have already told your mother this." He reached out and took my hand while I sat, paralyzed. "Clara." He leaned close. Our eyes locked, his breath steady, hovering just above my lips. My eyes fluttered shut. I felt as though nothing more out of the ordinary could possibly happen than for me to make out with our loyal houseman as if our plane was going down. But he didn't kiss me. Instead, he said, "*I quit.*" He moved back. "I am leaving the United States and going home." Axel then opened his door and left the car. "Get out. I have a lot to do."

He shut the door. I watched him walk out of the garage, hitting the button on the wall; the door rolled closed behind me. He opened the side door, the afternoon sun blinding me as he shut the door behind him, leaving me in the stuffy, stagnant heat.

I didn't move, didn't say a word. Raven had quit me, but now Axel? A few moments passed, and the garage security light timed off. I continued to sit in the pitch black, a tiny green light on the garage door button the only decipherable glow. The precious remnants of mechanical air mixed with the stuffiness of the garage, and I yawned. What was happening to my life? Axel can't move back to Argentina, and did he say he loved me? As in *loved* me? In which case, I *did* need him to move to Argentina because I just don't think of him like that. Although, I was just about to make out with him in the garage like a teenager. Or was I?

My head was spinning. Craving the company of Raven, I reached into my bag and picked up my phone. The screen saver, a picture of

Mom and Dad smiling, made my stomach lurch. It was nearly two o'clock. I wiped my eyes and dropped my phone back into my bag. And then, the relief I felt knowing something was suspicious about the review, combined with the lingering effects of too much alcohol and sleep aid, or whatever, took its toll, and I fell dead asleep, face down on the center console.

I wanted to be awake, yet I was being pulled into the depths of this green icky slime of a dream. I could feel it as it poured over me. It was neither hot nor cold but a degree below lukewarm and reminded me of street sludge. I felt my lips tighten, desperate not to let the oozing stuff inside of my mouth. In deep, thick echoes, I could hear myself nearly pounding in my ears. "You're disgusting! You are a fool! Look how you failed!" My emotions prompted me to scream. But I couldn't interrupt, lest the slime gets inside me. And just before I was forced to open my mouth, I found myself transported into a field, with my mother beside me.

"Breathe, Clara. Breathe," she whispered.

I could hear violin music. And she softly spoke the words our family used so often, a French melody of argument. *"In lieu of this..."*

But she left me no option.

I had no idea what time it was or where I was when I woke. Disoriented, I stretched and yawned; my blouse clung to my sweaty armpits and torso, drool dripping off my chin. The stifling heat of the dark garage further confused me, the only visibility offered by the tiny green light coming from the illuminated garage door button. I remembered Raven, telling me she could no longer treat me. Axel, saying I wasn't a good friend and that he was leaving. And Dad. Always, I remember, Dad. I laid my head back, groggy from the hard nap. The meeting with Lance had encouraged me some anyway. But dealing with the repercussions of forgetting to meet Axel for dinner, that was going to be a thing. I still had a desperate itch to text Raven and ask her if I could have just one more session. I just didn't have the clarity I needed to beg Axel to stay.

The idea of him going, I couldn't fathom, couldn't bring myself to even consider losing any more than I already had. Perhaps—no, for sure, I *had* taken advantage of Axel, had counted on him beyond his paygrade and traipsed all over our *friendship*. He asked for this favor, something he had never done before, and I neglected him. I raised my head, but a quick burning, prickly feeling came over me. *Something was not right.*

The little green light from the garage button suddenly disappeared. I could see nothing in the placid environment of the closed garage. Where had the light gone? If someone was standing in front of the button, the motion detector security light would have come on. I sat very still, and then, the light reappeared. I gasped, horror clutching my chest, as the shadow cast by a large figure stepped toward the car and slowly headed toward the passenger side of the car, right where I was sitting. My heart pounded against my ribs; a whisper escaped me. "*Shit.*"

The car windows were heavily tinted, but I feared this person had seen me through the windshield based on where he'd been standing. Unless it was too dark? Maybe he didn't know I was in the car. I slid my hand to the door latch and hit the lock button.

Click.

The figure stopped.

I could barely make out the silhouette when I heard another *click*. The door unlocked itself, activating the car's interior light.

Terror slithered over me as I remembered the extra key fob that hung on the wall under the dimly lit garage controller. Whoever this menacing figure was, *he had a key to the car.* Worse, he had done something to the security light.

Adrenaline surged, begging me to move while simultaneously paralyzing me. A flash of light hit my eyes, and I scampered to the driver's side and clawed and grabbed at the steering wheel, panic clutching my throat, making my screaming attempts faulty and pathetic. A single hand in a horrifying, menacing blue latex glove gripped my arm, yanking me from the car. He wrenched my arm behind my back in one deft movement, and I whimper-screamed my rebuttal.

He slammed shut the car door; then, shoving me up against the car, he leaned his hot, onerous body against me, and I was overcome with the blistering terror and the sharp pain of something jabbing into my ribs. Still unable to see anything but the blinding murk, I tensed at my petrifying deduction—the sharp object could only be one thing. A hefty, jagged knife. Salty tears blurred my vision further, running past my parched lips, offering no moisture to help me swallow or speak. I just panted like a trapped dog steeped in blinding horror in the darkness.

"Shhhhhhhhh," his hot breath whispered into my ear. I winced as angry chills ran over me. As I struggled with waning energy, feeling the weight of this monster like a brick wall against me, he grew in viciousness. The beast pressed harder into my side with the sharp weapon—a warning to obey. A muffled sob escaped me, sounding like it came from someone else. Someone feeble, someone I did not know. A warm stream of blood pooled down my side as he nearly lifted me off my feet while pulling even harder on my arm, nudging the blade deeper into my ribs. "Hello, *Honey.*" His voice was deep and terrifyingly wicked, with a Brooklyn accent, and his toxic breath reeked of chipotle and garlic. He lay his forehead on mine, rocking his head back and forth as if we were in some tender exchange. My stomach dropped; I felt my bowels lurch and cramp. His face brushed against my cheek, and I could feel the covering of a stocking or toboggan.

"*Hoooneeey,*" he mockingly purred. "*You have been noooosy. I have friends that don't like nosy little girls. So, they asked me to show you what happens when you go snooping around.*" The menace raised his weapon away from my side, and I was both shocked and horrified as the pressure subsided and I felt my warm, scarlet life source soak my blouse. His depraved laugh rang in my ears, and I was unable to withhold a shudder as the blade's tip pressed against my throat.

I moved slowly, and then, with all that I could muster, *wham!* I leveled my knee against his groin. Instead of feeling the soft give of unprotected flesh, a jolt of searing pain radiated from my knee and up my leg, which further disoriented me. I bent in agony and clutched at my bruised joint.

More laughter filled the garage, bouncing off the walls in a menacing bark. His closed fist slammed into my face with such force, I felt an earring fly off, landing in bouncing clicks, followed by the slap of my palms and the bone-breaking pain of landing on the harsh epoxy-concrete floor. The metallic taste of blood filled my mouth and began spewing from my nose. I was too shocked to move. The intruder grabbed at me in the dark, flipping me on my back, and then punched me in the stomach. Waves of pain and nausea followed. I lay collapsed on the floor, gasping for air. *Helpless.*

The brute grabbed my hair. Pulling me up to my knees, he rammed his knee into my ribcage three times. The wind gushed from my lungs, and blood and mucus choked me as he delivered blow after blow to my torso. I collapsed onto my back, the attacker crushing my hand under his enormous boot. I finally caught enough air and cough-whimpered,

"*Please…*" He just enclosed my throat in his Latex hand; again, his deep laugh bounced off the walls of the oven-like garage.

He tightened his grip. I limply struggled to loosen his fingers from around my windpipe with my free hand as the last of my strength drained away, the other still held defenseless under his boot. *I'm dying…* With the suffocation came blind panic. I could feel myself trying to flail. In my head, I released a scream: *Help!* But no sound or air escaped me.

Suddenly, he released my neck and grabbed my hair again, pulling my head back and pushing his blade into my throat.

"Aww, Honey, you didn't think a pro would come to teach you a lesson and not wear a cup, now, did you?" A jolt of pain shot from the base of my neck, and consciousness begged me to relinquish my hold. Limp and defeated, I prayed, *Just kill me.*

Bang!

A loud noise, followed by a harsh chemical smell, assaulted my senses, and then the burn of…*something. What was that?* The air I needed was thick with heat and a poisonous burn. I heaved it into my lungs, choking and gasping from the toxic oxygen wafting around me and the gurgling blood emptying from my mouth and nose. I heard more screaming and then another thud. With the loathsome boot finally off my hand, I slid my hands up the side of the car, desperate to stand and flee into the fresh air and home. But the harsh chemical fumes forced me back down, my eyes and throat in agony.

"*Heeeelllp…!*" The word emerged in a jagged, barely audible whimper that wouldn't have alerted a mouse as to this nightmare.

Still unable to get on my feet, I began crawling on all fours toward a glimmer of light—the evening sky, I assumed—and the open side door of the garage. I had crawled no more than a foot when I felt the crash of

IN LIEU OF EATING

something heavy against the back of my head. I collapsed to my belly with a thump. I heard a struggle taking place somewhere close, but with each moment, I grew more helpless, fading into surrender.

A shrill scream jolted me again, and panic forced me back up on all fours to crawl again. Only now my exit was further blurred by my tears and the blood. I was stopped again and yelped as my leg and ankle were repeatedly stomped on. This time, my already battered head smacked face-first onto the unforgiving concrete. The scuffle continued. Grunts, screams, and then, a deep voice and a muffled bellow laced with disturbing agony, followed by another thud.

Just before I gave in to pain and exhaustion, I heard a woman's frantic voice. "Honey! Honey! It's okay! Honey!"

I couldn't move; my eyes and throat were smoldering. I whimpered again for help. My rescuer scooped me up, cradling me on the hard, bloody floor, reassuring me, "It's okay, Honey! Stay awake!" The woman began to scream, "*Axel! Axel! Call 911!*" Followed by more, "It's okay, Honey," which came out in crackling sobs that contradicted her promise. She rocked me, purring, "I got you! *Don't go to sleep! Please…* help is coming. *Please, Honey,* don't go to sleep!"

In lieu of struggling, my body unable to combat the blood loss and head and neck trauma, I let go and slipped into darkness, safe in the arms of *Marcella*.

Fish Course

Slow motion. That's how I was falling. For the first time in months, I wasn't dreaming in blood-soaked images, plagued by visions of Leonard Pruitt screaming with my dad standing over him as the food critic begged for his life. But I wasn't dreaming now—I knew that much. I felt stiff and swaddled but safe. Everything in my current state of slumber—still oddly in slow-motion—was showered in the brightest of yellows. The bright white/golden light saturated me. My thoughts seemed not of my own. Occasionally, I would stir, and the yellow light would be invaded by harsh, blue lights—metallic in nature—followed by the stiff, antiseptic smell people associated with injury. But then, after the stirring would come a lovely warmth, filling my veins with numbness, bringing release from the pain.

In those moments, the finest of hairs all over my body would seem to hum in sync, and I could not wait to go back under. It was as if I floated on my back into the amber waves of thick breathlessness, the light, a thick gold liquid, crept over me. Every sensation of being fed radiated a reminder: *Notice! Wake up! Fight back! Live…"*

But I was happy in the yellow light. I just wanted to stay there a while longer.

The heart monitor, with its beeps breaking the silence, tickled at my consciousness until I could no longer ignore it. It nudged me awake. My eyes were swollen, but through the slits, I could see a large window and bright New York skyline, blue daylight its backdrop. I tried to sit up, but electrifying pain kept me still. Inadvertently, I moaned; my hoarse complaint was met with the welcomed French accent of my mother.

"*Darling!*" She rained kisses on my cheeks.

I groaned in defiance. *Everything* about me hurt.

"I am so sorry!" She wept. "I didn't mean to hurt you. Are you okay? Can I get you something?"

"Water," I whimpered.

I heard my mom bustle about, then felt the straw placed on my bottom lip. I opened my mouth to accept the straw, relief enfolding me instantly. The water was so cold, and my throat hurt so badly, I wanted to just keep drinking. But even the effort of holding my head up and using my mouth muscles proved exhausting, and I fell back onto the plastic crunch of hospital sheets, panting from my efforts.

"What... happened?"

"Don't speak." Mother's voice sent waves of adrenaline through my already burning veins. If I could move, I would crawl into her lap and stay forever.

"Mom, *please*," I whisper-pled. "What happened?"

She nervously tugged my blanket up, and I grimaced. The touch of the sheets even hurt.

Mom looked wrought with suffering, though I could barely see her face.

"Marcella." A sob escaped her. "I was looking for you. I had been calling… You didn't answer. Bo went looking on foot, thinking maybe you went to the bodega or coffee house. Axel had gone for a run and then to the gym. *I couldn't reach him.*" She whimpered, "I didn't know where you were." Her voice cracked with the recollection. "Marcella said she needed a bag out of the trunk of the car. Axel called just as she went out…"

I suddenly remembered; Axel wouldn't have realized I hadn't gone inside the house. And the chances that Marcella would fetch something for herself were slim to none. My head was beginning to spin as I pieced together snapshots of what had happened. Had the attacker been in my home? If I had gone into my flat, would there have been anyone to hear me? I closed my eyes. What if my sister hadn't come out to the garage? I inhaled a jagged breath.

"Marcella?" I sputtered. "Is she…?" I swallowed. "*Water…*"

Mom lifted the straw to my lips again, and I grabbed hold eagerly.

"Don't speak, love," Mother cooed. "Marcella is okay, but she did get a bad burn from the mace. She broke four fingernails, and…" She stopped. "You should rest."

"What? Mother, please, *what?*"

Mother inhaled. "Marcella is not badly injured. Her wrist is sprained, and her face is bruised. And… She… Well, she…" Mother composed herself, then tried to keep her voice steady. "The man…" She cleared her throat. "Your sister saved you by stabbing the attacker with her *red-bottomed Christian Louboutin shoe.*"

I would have laughed, or maybe cried, but I had no emotion left. "I'll have to pay her back for that."

"Yes, dear." My mother stroked my hand. "For the rest of your life, you will be indebted to Marcella."

IN LIEU OF EATING

I closed my eyes, exhaustion and pain lulling me back under before uttering my last words for the next twelve hours, a saying my dad always used:

"Who-da thunk it?"

Two days later, I was released from the hospital. I lay on the couch in the den of my parents' home on an ice pack, my wounds better but not any fun, my mind vaguely clearer. Lance and Lolly Vega had come by the hospital with our family lawyer, Rose Merchant, and some police investigators eager to check on me and find out what I knew about the attack. I knew nothing. The attacker was still unidentified, but Lance and the police felt strongly that the horrific incident had something to do with the murder of Leonard Pruitt. Primarily because of the few words spoken during the ambush in the garage.

"I have friends that don't like nosy little girls. So, they asked me to show you what happens when you go snooping around."

There was hope, or at least, I had sensed something in the Vegas' voices alluding to a connection. In the meantime, the attack was being kept out of the press, and we were to stay together at home until they knew more. There would be a police car on our street and in the alley for now, which made all of us feel better.

Safe at home, I felt out of my element, like a stranger in a foreign family game room/den. The phantom had suggested I was snooping. But regarding what? Although my attacker was now dead, I had no closure. Who sent him? I needed to talk to my sister. Yet another unusual experience as I hadn't needed or wanted to talk to my sister since about 1984. I hadn't seen or heard from Marcella since the garage, though I had left no less than fourteen messages for her. Bo and Davy were at school, and Mother's violin wafted soft French melodies through the house. A common and familiar ritual: Mother's daily practice of her beloved instrument. I flipped through channels, stopping occasionally on the news. Perhaps in the hope there would be some report, some connection to my attack and my dad's case. But nothing appeared, and nothing clicked. Instead, the special reports and "This just in!" chatter only made things more confusing.

A knock at the open, den door jolted me from my daze.

"Oh, hey, Axel." I greeted him and gingerly moved my feet for him to sit on the overstuffed, plaid sofa.

Axel looked defeated as he had all morning. His shoulders slumped, a sheepish frown on his face. He opted for the ottoman, sitting on the tufted edge, leaning on his knees. He nervously twisted his hat in his hands.

"I am so sorry, Honey." His voice quaked.

"For what?"

"I had no idea you were still in the garage." He shook his head. "I am worthless."

"Don't be a drama queen," I snorted. "You couldn't have known."

"I am not going back to Argentina. I mean, I will. But not now. I will stay on until your mom can find a new home manager and bodyguard."

"Bodyguard?" I scoffed. "We don't need a bodyguard. We just need more *red-bottomed Christian Louboutin* shoes."

Axel didn't laugh. He stood and walked to the window. Without turning around, he spoke, "Your dad knew I had eyes for you. He was always teasing me, *Honey needs a ride, wink-wink*. I guess I spent a lot of time focused on you, the idea of a life with you, on running things for Tom and Sylvie. I forgot to create a life for myself, forgot to seek anything that would bring me happiness. Now it feels too late. All I do every day is take care of you and your family and run errands like some tragic housewife. And I failed at my job. I feel so weak, *so stupid*."

I knew I should say something, but no words came. Axel and I were friends, good friends. I guess there had been some past flirting, though not during the last couple of years. This second confession of his feelings mystified me. He is handsome and funny and so generous. But other than some playful teasing, I hadn't really noticed much more.

"Axel...," I began.

"Let me finish." He said it with authority. "I am going to stay in the city, move out of the carriage house and in here with you, your mother, Marcella, and the boys. I can stay in the guest room. That guy, Lance...?"

I nodded.

"Well, he has a theory. We need to stay in this house. Whatever Lance and the police are hinting at, well, it's dangerous. I was gonna go out to see Tom, but..."

I perked up, interrupting, "Dad will see you?"

"Yeah," he grunted. "He said he would anyway. He's my friend, you know?"

I nodded, at least as much as I was able, a tight cervical collar rigorously hampering my movements.

"But Honey, now Lance said I can't go out there. Tom has been moved."

"Moved?" I yelped and Axel moved to me, hushing me. I whispered, "*Moved where?*"

Axel shook his head; he was too close to me now, and I strained to look up at him. Recognizing my struggle, he sat back down on the ottoman. He looked over his shoulder down the hall, then leaned in and said, "I don't know. Lance said the police believe that Tom is in danger. But Lance also said that *moved* could just mean he is in solitary protection. Lance promised he would let us know something as soon as he does."

I was suddenly so sleepy; I wasn't sure I was even still awake. My eyes fluttered shut, and I felt Axel's finger gently touch my cheek. My eyes flew open, and he pulled his finger away, standing quickly, and shoved his hand in his slacks' pocket. "Anyway," he inhaled. "I will keep you posted. I know you are really hurt, Clara, but I want you to think about something. When this mess is over, when you are safe, you are going to have to choose a life for yourself. You may not notice…" He scoffed. "No, you *don't* notice life, love, adventure… You don't notice those wonderful things because you notice everything else." He paused as if checking the appropriateness of what he was saying. "And then you run yourself ragged trying to make things your way. You notice Marcella's screwups, you notice your dad's absence, you notice all the bad stuff, and you never stop and look around. You have everything. You can have even more."

I swallowed hard, my swollen eyes on his. My mother's perfect melody crescendoed through the house as my pounding chest added percussion, racing faster than Axel's deliberate inhale and exhale.

Axel spoke again, "I don't know what happened. I don't know how your dad could have done what he says he did to that food critic. But people do stuff when they are scared or upset or in danger. I am not one that would have pegged Marcella as a ninja, but when you were in danger, she was one." He snickered. "I believe you are so entirely focused on bad stuff, striving so hard to keep things the way you want them, you aren't aware of how much more there is. How much more you are."

I sniffled. Axel stepped closer to the couch and cautiously touched my cheek again, his hand calloused and warm. "No matter what, Honey." His eyes danced as he looked down at me. "No matter what, eventually you will have to choose to live. And I hope you will find happiness when you do." He wiped a tear from my bruised cheek. "I am so sorry I was not there for you. *I am so sorry.*" His booming voice buckled. "So, so sorry."

He slowly turned. And, I noticed, *he left.*

IN LIEU OF EATING

I still had not showered since the morning of the attack. Now it was nearly 3:00. Bo and Davy would be home within the hour, and I didn't want to alarm them with my tragic appearance. Mother had stopped playing the violin, and I could hear her moving around the kitchen. I sent her a text: *Going to take a shower.* In pathetically weak form, I made my way from the den to my childhood bedroom.

I stood in the hall in front of the heavy mahogany door, staring at the intricately carved roses and cherubs scrolled across the door frame. I had failed to acknowledge or even notice the gatekeepers to my childhood room for years. I had lived in this house since I was seven. Our parents purchased the glamorous home when Marcella had been nine. I recall, we had insisted on sharing the room with the "angel door." Nudging myself from that reminiscence, I put my bandaged hand on the oiled brass knob and turned it. Pain charged up my arm, and I winced as I released my grip.

Creaaak... The hinges squealed and complained. A sprinkle of dust played in the rays of afternoon sunlight peeping wanly through heavy, pastel-gingham drapes. Two white, canopied twin beds, a white nightstand between them, sat empty. I limped to mine, the closest of the two beds, and sat. The quilts on the beds, awash in identical damask patterns, had lost some of their colorful luster, muted by age. My quilt, a soft, sunny yellow, still contrasted notably to Marcella's brilliant, blooming pink bedding.

I reached for the lamp switch on the nightstand. The lamp, a porcelain ballerina, stood frozen in a timeless pose beneath a bell-shaped shade. The appliance's long-braided cord peeped out beneath the lacy trim. I tugged on the cord, recoiling again at the sharp pain—my new constant, obnoxious companion. The light flickered to life, and that's when I noticed some scribbles in purple marker atop the white, lacquered nightstand.

FISH COURSE

Marcella and Honey
Best Friends Forever.

"Hey."

The voice from the door startled me, but the cuff that held my neck stable prevented me from turning. So, I swiveled my upper body slowly toward the door. Marcella hovered in the doorway, her left arm in a Gucci-printed sling. In a gray New York Yankees t-shirt, baggy, faded jeans, hot pink Converse sneakers, and no makeup, she looked almost alien. Her short, bleached-blonde hair was hidden under a pastel-blue baseball cap. But even in the brim's shadow, I could see bruises encircling Marcella's eyes, a band-aid on her chin, a large red burn on her cheek, and a bulging, fat lip.

"Hey." My stomach lurched at the subtle exchange. This woman, *my sister,* saved my life. Not that I knew for sure the attack would have resulted in my death, though I don't remember gaining the upper hand at any point during the ambush.

"You look like shit," Marcella declared. She moved to sit next to me on the bed.

I nodded, "You look clean." I teased, "I came in here to shower. But the walk down the hall may have convinced me to stay stinky."

Marcella bounced her feet in a child-like motion, and I put my wounded hand on her knee to stop the nervous movement.

"Oh!" She covered her naked lips with her free hand. "Sorry, no sudden movements."

"It's okay. Every little thing hurts."

We sat motionless, consumed in the silence of our past, unsure how to treat each other in the present or future. I had no words, but I knew I needed to find some. After several moments, I gave Marcella all I could… I lay my head on her shoulder. We both sniffled, too proud to burst into tears and so far past a normal sisterly exchange, I felt we should introduce ourselves politely. Finally, she spoke, her voice hoarse with emotion.

"You do stink."

I lifted my head, and our eyes met. This close to my sister, with nothing but the lives she saved, mine and hers, in common, alerted me to the familiar beauty she shares with our mother.

"You saved my life, Marcella."

"Nah." She uncharacteristically did not boast. "You would have killed that son of a bitch." Her voice cracked. "You would have been fine."

"No. That isn't true. He was going to hurt me further if not kill me. You saved my life."

Marcella didn't argue, silenced by the humility of how close I had come to detriment.

"I guess," I continued, "unless we are really paying attention, we aren't aware of what we are truly capable of. I didn't know you were capable of such power, such courage."

Marcella wiped a tear from her cheek with her free hand, and I noticed her battered nails and the cuts and scrapes that ran up her slim, smooth arm.

"I am sorry, Marcella."

"For what?"

"For not noticing how very competent and brave you are."

She scoffed, "Oh, please. You are just saying that. You would have done the same."

I pondered this, unsure if she was correct. My own historical words radiated in my head: *I am not chasing all over New York to look for my drunk sister. She can fend for herself!*

I decided to say it. "I wish I could say you are right, that I would have kicked an assailant's ass to save you. But…" I struggled with the confession. "I don't know that I would have."

FISH COURSE

Marcella dropped her head, and a teardrop landed on her denim-covered leg. She snorted a chuckle. "Well, I don't blame you. Not much worth saving."

I touched her shoulder. "Please don't say that." I had started, and now I needed to finish. I inhaled a ragged breath. "Marcella, this is all on me. Axel pointed something out to me, something about my choices, what I make a habit of. Basically, I am controlling, and I am missing out on a lot of good."

"*Hmph*," Marcella huffed.

"What?"

"It's just cliché. I guess. The wise, loyal houseman, working on a specified wage, telling the millionaire mistress of the home, *You don't know what you're missing*."

"Maybe it's cliché. But maybe it's also spot-on."

Marcella nodded. "You do miss a lot. No matter how I've tried, it's like it's never enough."

I bit back a gasp. Am *I* being accused of self-absorbed behavior? By *Marcella*? I held up a maimed hand. "I don't understand. What is never enough? What are you talking about?" I stopped short of saying, *Tell me, Ms. ONE…COBALT…BLUE…SHOT…OF…TEQUILA!* Because I really did want to know.

"We were going to be a team. You were going to cook in my studio…" Her fractured voice trailed off. But I instantly remembered.

"Oh, yeah!" I said enthusiastically. "We were going to offer culinary classes and art classes at that old warehouse in the West Village!"

Marcella pursed her fat lip and nodded. "But then you started making plans with Dad. I couldn't get you to listen. I just wanted to be a part of what you were doing. Then it seemed the only time Dad invested in my work was if I somehow demanded it. And when I was messing up? He would sit and talk with me, like he does you. Only, if things were going well, I mean, if I was proud of something, something I wanted to share with my family, he didn't have anything to say to me. So, I started being more brazen, more crass. It was like, *that was my role*. Like, we are all just characters in *your show*, Honey the Great." Marcella stood and walked to a heavy, white-lacquered armoire. The piece, a familiar ghost from the past, had been custom-painted in Paris by an artist friend of Mother's family. Sunflowers, climbing ivy, rosy peonies, and dozens of bright-orange Monarch butterflies danced over the sturdy wood, captured in a timeless, clear, glossy finish. Marcella opened one door with her free hand, pulled out a folded piece of school notebook paper, and returned to sit on her childhood bed, opposite me.

She handed me the paper. My eyes were still swollen, and I didn't have my contacts in. I'd left my glasses on the coffee table in the den, but I could make out Marcella's loopy script in her signature, bright-red ballpoint ink.

"The morning before your grand opening event on 57th…" Marcella half-chuckled a whimper. "I wanted to talk to Dad about a toast before dinner at the event. I guess I thought, since it was a new beginning, maybe…"

I interrupted her, "Marcella…" My voice splintered, shame choking me. "Will you read it? I can't really see."

Marcella took the paper and began to read-perform, "Good evening, friends, thank you for joining our family tonight for this very special occasion. I wanted to begin by saying, it is not easy being the oldest sister of a genius-demigoddess. Perfection is always my goal. And when one has a goal, one must also have a measure by which to achieve that goal. *My measure is my sister, Honey.*"

I was speechless. What would I ever say to make amends for my wicked treatment of my sister, my oldest *friend*?

She continued. "Honey doesn't have competition. Honey from bees, that is. What is there that compares? Sugar cane, molasses, sticky maple syrup? There is just nothing like honey in nature. And my sister, Honey, excels by nature. She has no competition. She doesn't look behind her to see who is following, and she looks past those whom she will conquer. She doesn't recognize the competition because she only needs to exceed herself, her last greatest accomplishment. She is the perfect daughter. And I feel certain if we were friends…" She held up a long finger, her nail broken to the quick with a bloody scab running from her knuckle to her tiny wrist, signaling an imaginary audience. "*Pause for laughter.*" She lowered her finger. "We would be the perfect sisters. I am not sure that everyone seated in my little sister's five-star restaurant understands how very diverse and motivated Honey is. But what I know, what I am certain of, is the food you are about to be served will be the most exotic experience one can have in our fine city. *Pause, nod to mayor's table.*" She looked at me briefly, perhaps to try and gauge my response. "*Continue.* And if not, we can all wander over to Nobu 57." Again, she held up her battered finger. "*Pause for laughter. Continue.* Please raise a glass to my baby sister, Chef Honey."

The heat of my shame burned red hot across my belly and then up my neck, needling my cheeks and ears. Marcella folded the paper as blameworthy tears dripped off my chin.

She spoke again. "So, yeah, I wrote this. I sat down with Dad on the downstairs porch with a cup of coffee to talk. Dad immediately stood up and said, *Okay, baby girl, I'm going up to Honey's.* And kissed me on the cheek." Marcella's voice faltered, and her eyes stormed. "I could hear you. I sat on the porch, listening to you two right above me. You were laughing, both of you. And then you talked about the election and a play you saw with Axel. Then Dad went on and on about parking at the tennis club."

IN LIEU OF EATING

I tried to nod, my voice too ragged to speak, my neck too swaddled to move much. I remembered that morning and had a realization. *I had cherished that morning*, had relived it thousands of times since Dad confessed to Pruitt's murder. The last cup of coffee I had with my dad was the cup that my sister needed to have with *her* dad. The fact that she was sitting beneath us, that the weight of her rejection was literally hanging on a wooden frame just above her head, made my culpability taste even more pungent.

Marcella resumed her confession. "Sitting on the porch, this stupid tribute in my pocket, I thought, maybe I could lower my guard, ask how I can help? How I can work with you?" She stared at her hand, her breath low and soft. "But then, I heard Dad's roaring belly laugh over something you said, and I thought, *Oh, He doesn't like me…*" Her voice quaked and she mumbled, *"Dad doesn't like me."*

I gasped, facing my sister, my self-proclaimed enemy. We had united in empathetic awareness of how it feels to need Tom Honeycutt and have no real access to him.

Marcella stood, crumpling up the paper, and threw it in an archaic Boyz II Men trash can. I wanted to stop her but was unable to move. Marcella straightened her back, lifting her chin, determined to be strong. Which made her look even more vulnerable and desperate. My heart felt heavy in my chest; each beat echoed all the precious time wasted by not noticing my sister.

The words floated from Marcella with authority. "I know what you are thinking," she grunted. *"Why would Dad like me?* I stayed in character for so long, trying to win Dad over, to notice me. I guess it was too late." She sniffled and continued, "I can't even seem to connect with my own sons." She sat back at our childhood vanity and began messing with old tubes of glitter-drenched creams and bottles of designer perfumes. "I am afraid if I do, they'll see me for who I really am. I'd almost rather they hate me than be seduced into liking or needing me."

I felt as if I was back on the concrete floor, having just been violently kicked in the ribs. Marcella's suffering was so tangible, her reasons so coherent.

Marcella continued, "You know when I left, after Davy was born? I was *never* going to come back. I didn't want the boys to even know I existed. I thought, maybe I could make them believe I was dead. Because I knew, if I kept them, you and Dad would have never liked them." She said the words nonchalantly, dusting her nose with a big pink makeup brush.

I finally interrupted, "You thought we wouldn't like Bo and Davy?"

She nodded, eyeing me over her reflection. "I had wondered if you could ever be endeared to anything that was born of me. You look at me with such contempt, you know. I guess I believed that you would think Bo and Davy were ridiculous *like me*."

We sat in the quiet. Proper etiquette would have insisted I correct my sister, tell her she was wrong. Culture demanded I throw out pleasantries and synthetic accolades. *Don't be silly. Oh, you must have misunderstood.* But I had already taken so much from my sister. I refused to take anything more. Her interpretation wasn't spot-on, and certainly, there was tit for tat, equivalent accusations that could be leveled. But this was *her pain*, and she noticed it, she acknowledged it. She saw what was happening around her, and she responded.

"I am sorry" was all I could finally muster.

Marcella kept messing with her face and then, something shifted. I saw it immediately, in her stance, the change in her eyes—a glint in them.

She dabbed some cream on her cheeks. "Well, half of my pedigree is of royal French descent. The other half's only real claim of esteem involves partial ownership in a franchise of a Dairy Queen."

I belly-laughed, clutching my wounds. "Marcella!" I scolded.

She turned on the tufted vanity chair and looked at me, cocking her head in that old, haughty way. "I think that after Dad killed Pruitt, I got free of needing him. I think it is the greatest favor he ever did for me."

I was too shocked to speak, realizing, at that point, that Marcella believed Dad was guilty. I hadn't ever even discussed it with her.

She turned back around and continued to primp. "Hmph," she whispered. "I seem to have left you speechless. Another pleasant outcome." She flicked a gaze at me over her shoulder.

I wanted to say something quick, clever, and cutting, but I felt done. A weird sense of resolve settled into me. I didn't have to agree with Marcella, but it felt comfortable and safe in that room, just sitting with her. No debating, no competition. I thought about Emo Pruitt's observation: *Marcella is funny… I have always enjoyed her mind.*

"Hey, Marcella?"

She turned again to face me, teenaged makeup creating bursts of creamy color on her face, accentuating her bruises. "Yeah?"

I blurted out a giggle; she looked fifteen. "Hey, the night that Dad threw me the surprise party…?"

"What about it?" she asked flatly, her guard up.

"I saw Mother and Dad fighting in the corner of the main dining room. Do you know what they were arguing about?"

She turned away again, picked up a glass bottle and sprayed a big puff in the air, sniffing it and then scrunching her nose in repulsion. She snickered and then looked back at me in the reflection. "Yeah." She stood and walked to the door. I turned my body to face her as she remarked, "You know, it's a wonder the universe conspired for me to go out to the garage. You are an awful lot like him."

"Dad?" I questioned.

She rolled her battered eyes. "Yeah. And yeah, that was a rough night, *it being Mother's birthday and all.*"

"Oh, my God! Wait, *what?*" I gasped.

Marcella adjusted her sling and lifted her chin. "I don't want to negate our newfound *friendship* with a sharp tongue. But there's nothing you could do about it in your condition anyway. You are an ass, Clara Honeycutt. Dad is an ass. For whatever reason, I adore you both."

She turned and shut the door. I sat there, gazing at the makeup splayed across the vanity top, then peering at my face held rigid above my neck cuff. And the revelations came, one after the next. I wanted to be kinder to my sister, less controlling, less driven by all that I hated and really start living, in lieu of festering.

First Main Course

Truth be told, I wasn't going to be showering by myself. So, I succumbed to my injuries and slowly made my way back to the den. Halfway down the hall, I stopped to lean and rest when I heard the doorbell. There was a clamor of, "I'll get it!" and then the soft murmur of voices: Axel's, Marcella's, Mother's, and others I couldn't decipher. My mother floated around the corner and announced, "Honey, Lance Vega and Rose Merchant are here to speak with us."

Mother helped me limp into the den. Axel and Lance and Rose appeared and rushed over to help.

"I'm okay," I assured them.

The entire gathering fussed over my seat, fluffing throw pillows, offering me various things like a cushion for my bandaged foot, a cool beverage, a hot beverage… I think someone offered to paint my bedroom. Unable to stomach much more baby talk or sympathy, I interrupted the cacophony. *"Please!"* Quickly, I softened my brittle voice. "Please. I'm okay. Everyone, *please.*"

Mother ignored me and pulled a forest-green cashmere throw off my great-great-grandmother's heirloom rocking chair. She tucked it around me. She then sat down, so close, she was nearly in my lap, next to me on the couch. A tiny groan escaped me, and she patted me on my shoulder.

Lance leaned forward, opening a file folder. "Okay, guys, we don't have much. But we think we have something."

Rose continued, "We met with the district attorney and the police. They believe that Tom's confession was suspicious, but as a member of his legal team, I can confirm he will not recant his admission of guilt."

Lance looked at Rose with a *Tell them* side-eye. I don't know how old Rose is, but I don't have any memories of her *not* being our lawyer. She's like a family heirloom, always around. She has a 1950s bleach-blonde hairstyle and small, smart-looking glasses. Rose always wears a black pantsuit paired with one of a menagerie of brightly colored geometric printed blouses she apparently kept in her closet. When I was very young, I once asked her, "Ms. Merchant, Is that the same suit every day? Or do you have a bunch of them?" She didn't answer, which I took as a definite, *It is the same suit.*

Rose spoke with calm determination. "Well, Tom, *your dad…*" She motioned to me and Marcella. "He did speak with me, although it was brief. He has a message…*for Honey.*" I watched Marcella's soul shrink, my sister's face pinched and contorted with her unmet needs. For just a moment, I was angry at my dad. Why would he be so cruel? I shook the thought out of my head. But I felt itchy. I wanted to do something, take some action to help my family. My neck, inhibited in the trauma cuff, and my heavily bandaged and barely pliable joints didn't exactly facilitate my need for fast action. I would have to tend to my sister's hurts later. I turned my attention back to Rose, and my voice crackled to life, "What? What did he say?"

Lance pulled a piece of paper from the file and handed it to me. I squinted and strained as no meaning sprung forth from what had been written on it.

10R 18L 44R

Marcella begged, "What does it say?"

"*10R 18L 44R*," I read out loud.

"Do you know what that is?" Lance asked.

"I don't know." Anger bubbled up. What the hell was Dad doing to us? "*I don't know!*" I spat. "I don't know what is going on!" Unable to contain everything I felt, the frustration, the months of knowing nothing, I ranted, "I hate him! This is not a game!"

Rose cooed at me, "Clara, calm down. Let's keep our wits. Do those numbers mean anything to any of you?"

"Yes," Marcella quietly answered. We looked at her in desperation. She sighed, rolling her eyes, then shot a glare at my mother, who sat quietly, saying nothing.

Marcella continued, "It's Mom's birthday! October 18, 1944. It's probably a locker combination. *10R 18L 44R*."

I pushed away the childish thought, *Well, aren't you a wizard!* I replaced it with, *I am an ass.* In my defense, I did know that my mother's birthday was in October, but come on. I'm expected to recall the exact date and year too?

"Do any of you know where he might have a locker or safe? Anything you can think of that would advance our investigation?" Lance inquired.

"That isn't the combination to the home safe," Mother answered stiffly, and I turned my torso to stare at her, confused by her lack of participation up to this point.

"No," I agreed. "And it isn't the combination to the safe at the restaurant or the office."

Marcella tilted her ball cap up a bit, exposing further the beating she'd received in her efforts to save me. "I bet it's his tennis club combination. In the men's locker room?"

Lance snapped his fingers and pointed at Marcella. "Yup! I bet that is it!"

"No, no," Axel interjected. "I retrieved Tom's things from the club after he was in custody. And those lockers have keypad locks, not spinners."

I was incensed and again wondered what in the hell Dad was doing. "I can't do this anymore." I said it blankly.

"What is it, dear?" Mother begged.

"I need a shower and to clear my head. And I feel like…" Sweat began to bead on my lip, and nausea teased, *You are going to blow…* I looked at Marcella, hoping she could read my distress. She was up in a flash, a brass garbage can at my chin just before the bloody mucus, water, and green bile—all infused with the heady smell of narcotics—purged from me so barbarously, I thought I might suffocate. Once again, the crowd fussed. I was too compressed by my dressings and disoriented to argue.

Finally, Marcella demanded, "I need to get my sister cleaned up and horizontal. Excuse us."

Marcella guided me to the bathroom located off our childhood bedroom. Axel and Mother had already gone to my flat to retrieve clean pajamas and some of my other things as promised. I noticed fresh yellow underwear and a neatly folded pair of silky red pajamas, decorated with fine, hand-stitched cherry blossoms. I whimpered, "Marcella, if I am going to die, I want to be buried in those pajamas."

She giggled, then sat on the edge of the tub, turned on the faucet, and tested the water. "You're such a drama queen. You aren't dying." The irony of Marcella scolding me over my drama should have ignited some crude rebuke, but instead, I stood there, vulnerable and nearly helpless as my sister began to undress me.

I tried not to look in the mirror, having avoided all reflective surfaces since I woke up in the hospital. But when Marcella bent, struggling to remove my sock and trauma boot with her lone, uninjured hand, I caught myself in the mirror. I wasn't shocked that I looked like I'd been locked in a cage with Mohammed Ali. I was, however, stunned over how much I no longer looked like my dad.

My bulging purple eye sockets only allowed for a tiny sliver of my turquoise-blue pupils to peep through. My right eyeball was nearly black with blood. My lips were dry and swollen, with a few oddly menacing, prickly sutures winding from the middle of my bottom lip down to the curve in my chin. With the cervical collar now removed, bruising and a scabbed cut were visible on my neck. Streaks of blue-green, yellow, and purple bruising ran down my chest and arms. I stood there motionless, completely exposed as my sister put a shower cap over my bandaged head.

"You look like crap." Her frail attempt at relaxed humor fell a bit short. "I will have to get you an appointment with Dr. Santee in Los Angeles when this mess is over. While he is fixing your lip, maybe he can straighten your nose. Of course, genetics, not the beating, is to blame for that Honeycutt honker, but he could straighten the bump out from your skiing debacle." I heard the nervousness in her voice as she chattered on. "We can't wash your hair—"

I interrupted, "I will give you my Bono-autographed copy of the U2 concert tour CD if you will help me wash my hair."

She took my elbow and guided me into the hot tub. "Well, that is a tempting offer—or it would be, to someone who hadn't already had dinner with the band, *in her home*, after the concert." She lowered me gently into the gloriously scalding-hot water. "But you know, I still have ink on my ass from a more private autograph signing party." She handed me a bar of soap. "Scrub your pits, sis."

She moved to lean against the vanity as I scoured the remnants of terror from my battered flesh. "You're lying," I snorted. And in one slick

FIRST MAIN COURSE

move, Marcella unbuttoned her 501s and flashed her smooth left butt cheek, revealing an autographed tattoo: *Love 4ever, Bono.*

Cackling in painful waves of laughter reminiscent of baths gone past, my sister helped me bathe. And again, I noticed her. Marcella's wit, her compassion, and her deep need to be needed, mingled with the fog of the steamy bathroom.

Mother eventually came in to expedite the bathing and dressing process and brought me back to the safe and welcome rest offered by the den. I had just closed my eyes when Axel tapped on the open door again.

"Clara?"

I couldn't even lift my head, my eyes heavy from the exertion of simply bathing and dressing. "Yeah."

"I need to talk to you." He sounded too serious. I had hardly said, "Okay," when he began. "I think I might know what the combination is for."

Suddenly energized, I yelped, "What?"

"I think it is for an old, blue lock box at the warehouse. I remembered seeing it when your dad and I moved some chairs from the restaurant. Anyway, I didn't know if you wanted to tell Lance, or…" He cleared his throat. "Do you want me to go get it?"

I grabbed his arm, wincing as my sprained fingers clutched his suit coat. "*Please.*"

"Okay," he shuffled his feet, hands buried in his pants pockets. "Your mother is busy with Bo and Davy in the kitchen. Marcella is lying down in your parents' room. I'll be back in a couple hours. Traffic will be rough this time of day." He turned to go, and I called to him.

"Axel!" He stopped and looked at me, raising his trim eyebrows inquisitively, and my heart bounced violently against my bruised ribs. "*Please, be careful.*"

No sooner than Axel had gone, and I closed my eyes to finally rest, that my mother's voice alerted me to another visitor. "Honey, darling?" she purred.

I lay still, not sure what kind of a beating a girl had to take to get a nap in this house.

"Raven is here to see you." With every ounce of energy left in me, I pulled myself up to a sitting position as Raven stepped into the den.

"Oh!" Raven grieved, "Honey, my goodness!" Tears poured down her brown cheeks, and her locks clicked against my splinted arm and cervical cuff as she gently bent to hug me. "Your mother called me." Her voice was uncharacteristically shaky. "I am so sorry, Clara. I didn't have any idea. It wasn't on the news." Suddenly her face morphed, and I realized quickly her concern. A sexual assault would not have been reported with my name.

"No, no." I spoke, "He didn't." I cleared my throat. "Marcella stopped him. She killed him, Raven."

Raven's eyes were wild with shock. I filled in some gaps and then explained, "He said he was sent to teach me a lesson. The police are keeping everything on the down-low. They aren't sure if this is connected to Dad." My head was suddenly pounding, and I had to lie down, lest I fall off the sofa. "I'm sorry," I breathed. "I need to lie back."

"Yes!" Raven stood, her beads and scarves fluttering as she helped me lie down. Maternally, she picked my glass up off the coffee table and guided my lips to sip from the straw.

I scooted my butt over, and she sat next to me. Resting her long fingers gently on my sternum, she closed her eyes as if to pray and took several deep breaths. I just lay there, in the foreign, intimate company of a woman I admired but who could no longer be my therapist and was too professional to be my friend.

FIRST MAIN COURSE

"You were right," I whimpered. Raven's thick lashes fluttered open, and she folded her hands in her lap. We did not speak for several moments, and then I continued. "I missed everything good by noticing everything bad. As much as I love you, as much as I thought coming to you was saving me…" My throat tightened. "It was just a different venue for the same drivel. But I apologize. I hope you know, you saved my life."

Raven shook her head. "No, I didn't advance you. I am the one who is sorry."

I raised my voice a bit. "*You did*. Moreso after the fact. Letting me go, calling me out. I know that is not your brand of therapy. I know, you wanted to see me through." My words sounded as if years had passed between us, though it had only been days. But those few days had changed everything.

Raven nodded. "I couldn't let my pride get in the way. I did want to see you through. I like you. But letting you go was right for you. Honey…" She lay her hand on mine. "Promise me you will still seek some help. Especially now."

"I promise," I drowsily swore. I don't remember her leaving. I didn't say goodbye, falling asleep at some point. Somewhere in the fog of rest, I knew, I would never see Raven again. And it was okay. I was okay.

So, I slept, in lieu of all else, and dreamed of sunflowers, rain, and a rusted, little lockbox on a shelf in the warehouse.

When I woke, I could hear Axel's and Bo's voices carrying over from the kitchen. I started to holler, but my throat was on fire, dry grit caking my tongue. My joints felt as if they had turned to stone. For the first time in ages, I felt no urgency, no fear. And although nearly every part

IN LIEU OF EATING

of my body hurt, I felt rested and safe. It wasn't long before footsteps thumped toward the den, and I mustered out, "*Axel?*"

Moments later, we were turning the combination on the dusty metal box he had retrieved from the warehouse, just as Marcella walked into the room.

"What's that?" she inquired.

Click.

I looked at her with steely intent and said, "The combination…? The numbers Dad sent?" Marcella nodded. "It's the combination to this box." I tapped the top.

"What's in it?" she begged as I opened the box. Inside was a heavy brass key and a single piece of paper with the address: 1111 West Park Avenue PH1 scribbled on it. I removed the items, and Axel set the box on the coffee table. My ears rang and my breath quickened. With Marcella and Axel hovering over me, I picked the paper up and read the address again out loud.

"1111 West Park Avenue, Penthouse 1."

"Oh, shit. I think that's the building Pruitt lived in," Axel gasped.

"What makes you think that?"

"I know that building." He opened his phone, and after a few moments, he turned the screen to face us. "Yeah! See? That's a picture of Leonard's daughter making a statement to the press outside his apartment."

Marcella snorted. "He didn't live in the penthouse."

"How do you know?" Axel asked.

"I've been to a party at Emo's in that building. Leonard did live there. He and Emo had condos next to each other. It's nice, beautiful," Marcella explained. But I know it wasn't the penthouse." She opened her phone and scrolled. "Yeah, see here." Marcella showed us her contact and read, "Emo Pruitt. Owner, operator, Purple. 555-344-4545. 1111 West Park Avenue, number 9B."

Axel nodded, "No, not the penthouse."

"We should go there," I said flatly.

"Go where?" My mother's voice startled us, and I shut the box and Marcella stepped in front of us.

Marcella covered, "Oh, we were just talking about a restaurant that Axel tried."

Mother looked at Marcella suspiciously and then said, "Well, I'm ordering takeout tonight. Axel, would you please run and pick it up?"

"Of course, Sylvie," he said as he followed her into the hall.

"Why did you do that?" I asked.

"She can't know," Marcella answered, then moved to the loveseat and sat.

"She can't know we have a lead and that there is hope for getting Dad out?"

Marcella shook her head. "Wow. You are oblivious."

Exasperated, I begged, "Marcella, please, just tell me what you are alluding to."

"Oh, my God!" Marcella squawked. "You are such a bitch!"

My jaw tightened. I wanted to lay Marcella out, punch her in the face. It mixed oddly with my previous emotions, since a few minutes ago, she was helping me shave my legs—not to mention that she saved my life a few days ago.

"Damnit, Marcella! Just tell me what is going on!"

She folded her arms and narrowed her gaze. "Honey, Leonard Pruitt was Mom's lover."

I stared at her as the room flip-flopped, and my head followed. "Huh?" was all I could muster.

"*Huh?*" Marcella mocked. "Yeah, stupid. Where have you been?" She snorted and continued. "I would guess, although I am not the genius you are, the penthouse on West Park was their *space*." Marcella adjusted her sling, then looked at her nails and frowned. "Geez, Lexi needs to get here quick and fix my nails."

My brain was glitching between Mom's lover and my sister's manicurist. "What are you even talking about?" I demanded.

Marcella moved to the door, and with an exasperated huff, grumbled, "You know, I need to get some air and text Lexi. Maybe you and *your* mother should have a little chit-chat before you go rifling through her dead lover's sex shack." And she left.

I sat in the den considering my sister's words and actions. She hadn't really changed. She had just done this thing that helped me *one time in our freaking lives.* Romanticizing her wasn't going to make her any less Marcella. I fumed at the idea of my mother being disloyal to my dad. They loved each other. Didn't they?

And if my mother was having a torrid affair with a food critic, wouldn't Axel have known? He drove Mother everywhere.

At that moment, Axel stepped into the den. "Hey, I am back with food. Your mom ordered—"

I cut him off. "Did you know?"

"Know what?"

"Did you know that my mom and Leonard Pruitt were lovers?"

The look on Axel's face was testimony enough. Oblivion laced with utter shock.

"No way?" He laughed. "You aren't mixing merlot and codeine, are you?"

I stared at him. He stopped laughing and moved to sit on the ottoman close to me. "You're serious?"

"I don't know." Disbelief still nipped at me. "Marcella said that they were lovers. That the penthouse was Mother and Leonard's love nest."

"I don't know how Sylvie could get away with that. I take her to all her appointments. I am with her as much as I am with you." He paused. "Well, except Tuesdays, Wednesdays, and Fridays when she goes to…"

"Goes to *where?*" I begged.

Axel searched his mind. "I don't know. I can't remember. After your dad, well… It changed after Tom was arrested. But for at least eight or nine years, no? Ten years. I think, as long as I've worked for them, Sylvie never needed me on Tuesdays, Wednesdays, and Fridays."

"A tri-weekly sex meet-up?" I bellowed and Axel reached out and patted me.

"Clara, shhh. You don't want her to hear you."

"Yes!" I yelped. "Yes, I do! I want some answers!"

"We will get them." Axel patted me again. "But you need to rest now. Marcella could have just been trying to get under your skin."

I closed my eyes. All the madness I'd apparently missed in my family was now sneaking up and wringing my neck, *literally*. "Yes." I opened my eyes. "Marcella is still Marcella." I sighed, somewhat disappointed to know my sister is still an ass but willing to accept the spot-on branding if it meant my mom wasn't an adulterous liar.

"But…" I considered. "As much as I hate to admit it, Marcella probably knows more about what is going on than I do."

"I think you need to eat something and get some sleep. I will help you tomorrow. For now, let me bring you a taco and some ginger ale. After that, you can get some rest, and we will start fresh in the morning. Okay?"

"Okay," I said. And then, I did something ridiculous. I gently slipped my hand into Axel's. Both of my eyes were swollen from a colossal beating. I still don't know what came over me. But I did my best to shoot him what I thought were *bedroom eyes* and leaned in as if to kiss him.

"What are you doing?" He pulled away from me.

Embarrassed, I said, "Nothing. I, uh…"

Axel cut me off. "Clara, do not misconstrue what I said earlier for a new path for your addictions. I am not interested in you like that anymore."

Humiliation rose hot and red up my neck, illuminating my cheeks. Axel stood and said, "You have a long road ahead of you. Your body needs to heal, and you need a psychiatrist and an addiction group. I will help you get to the bottom of why all this came to a head. But I won't be involved in your continued quest to make other people make you happy, only to fail."

I rolled my eyes, both out of irritation and mortification.

"Don't," he spat. "You don't get to write a dialogue where I'm the jerk. I am moving back to Argentina. So, get the rest of it out of your concussed head. I'll go get your food."

Axel didn't return with my food, Bo did. He approached me with caution. "Aunt Honey?" His eyes widened when I turned to him. "Oh!" he gasped.

"Yeah," I said, trying to ease his shock. "I got my ass beat. You should see the other guy."

"You look like crap."

"You look like a Taco Shack delivery boy. Bring me that taco."

He put the tray on my lap and opened a can of ginger ale. "Do you want a straw?"

"No, thanks."

"Aunt Honey, Davy wants to see you. But I..."

I looked at him, a taco hovering near my mouth. "What?"

"I think I will distract him until bedtime. We can play Mario Kart in my room. I think it would be too upsetting for him to see you."

"Awww," I hummed. "You're a good boy." I switched to baby talk to lighten the mood. "Wooking out for your widdle bubba."

"Knock it off!" Bo rebelled and his voice cracked. "I'm being serious. I don't think he should see you like this."

Backing off even more from teasing, I bit into the taco and held back a gag. "I'm sorry." I crunched and chewed. "You're right."

"Do they know who did this to you?"

I shrugged and choked down more taco only to coat my stomach so I could take my medicine and go to bed. "No. But some pieces are coming together. It's going to be okay."

"Yeah." He nodded. "I won't make it worse for you."

"What do you mean?"

"I'm stepping up. I'm going to be a better man."

I snickered, which was not the right response, but I backed off a bit and giggled. "Oh, really?"

"Don't laugh!" he demanded. "I'm dead serious. I know the difference. I need to be the man of the house. If it was 1822, I'd be married with six kids working the fields."

"Working the fields?"

"You know what I mean." Bo shuffled his feet. "I'll be sixteen soon. Axel is going back to Argentina. I need to step up. Be there for Davy."

"You're a good guy, Bo."

"No." He shook his shaggy head. "No, I'm not. But I will be. You won't have to bail me out or lie to my teachers anymore. I'm telling you, Aunt Honey, I'm gonna be different. You can trust me from now on."

"I already trust you," I lied.

"Thanks," Bo said. "I'll take care of Davy. I hope you look better in the morning."

I laughed. "Don't you mean, *feel* better?"

"No." He shook his head, that wicked grin on his pimpled face. "No, I really do hope you look better."

And he left.

I set my empty plate down, reveling in the aftertaste of Tex-Mex instead of blood and tears. It was actually nice to have some food in my stomach. I swallowed a handful of pills and slowly made my way back to my old bedroom. As I shuffled down the hall, I forced any thoughts of my mother having an affair from my mind. I was too tired to think about it. And since I don't have a new therapist yet, I certainly didn't want to try to imagine it.

I climbed into the old bed, my landing spot for every childhood hope and dream. The crisp sheets welcomed me like a longed-for hug. I felt a bit of anger; if my mother and Leonard were lovers, had it driven my dad to murder him? I couldn't process any more tonight. I shut the light off and covered my head with the blanket.

I felt scared, out of touch. Confusion and humiliation battled for my attention. And on top of everything, what in the world made me think kissing Axel would clear a few things up? The door creaked; I couldn't face anyone at the moment. So, I lay still, pretending to be asleep.

Marcella tiptoed to her side of the room, turned down the blankets, and climbed into bed. And for just a moment, I felt it again. The warm yellow light, the amber gold, warmth, and comfort of noticing everyone I love, in lieu of missing everything.

Palate Cleanse

It was well after midnight when the house finally fell silent. I lay in my childhood bed, my sister in hers, just close enough so that I knew, *She's here. You're alive. It's okay.* My mind buzzed, chasing sleep away. How much have I missed, not noticed throughout the years? How many memories did I fabricate? Still wide awake, Marcella's steady breath and the hum of the air conditioner broke the silence, barely distracting me from my thoughts.

Then my mind drifted to bees, a pretty nonsensical thing to ponder, all things considered. Still, there they were, buzzing in my mind's eye. I questioned the validity of my trauma, which I guess is a normal reaction. Surprising, though, how I devoted so little regard now to the horrors that had seemed so tangible and life-threatening just hours ago. Instead, I thought of bees, their busy diligence, the hefty lengths they go to for the continuation of their species. Flashes of the attack and tinges of heartbreak and loss that had plagued me since my dad went to prison bantered now and then with the bees for my attention. But I was no longer consumed with those things.

What I return to in my mind now, instead of the carnage, the aftermath, is, rather, what I have learned in the last few months. In my brokenness, I see *humanity*. We, humans, are bees. Our strengths can be our greatest weakness, even unto our death. The "me" that I was before I wanted to start noticing things, before all the pain and loss, I no longer know. It's as if, in tasting death, experiencing that brutality of self—not that I in any way justify assault, especially on me—opened a glimpse into a doorway, a wink of the yellow light that has just kept growing. It's overtaking what was there before. The darkness. A bitter, toxic, self-deprecating cesspool of complaints and accusations. That place where I always had to be right and better.

The best, even if it meant twisting reality a bit, or manipulating others until I was superior, on top, and my opponent was leveled. Letting them have the last pleading words, *But Honey...*

Despite all that I knew, or thought I believed about my dad, what would happen if I were to suddenly learn otherwise? I grew more restless; all these unanswered questions swatted at the honeybees in my mind. I must have finally drifted off because I found myself in an empty auditorium. I looked around, recognized the space, and mentally assured myself, *It's just a dream.*

I studied my surroundings. This is where Marcella performed her one-woman show. Upon my recognition, the stage curtain swung wide, and my heart banged like the tribal drums in Marcella's one-woman act. I shook my head, willing myself to wake up—because truly I cannot sit through this again. The white horse came on stage, but this time the spray paint read: *Look up from your prep table, chef.* And Emo Pruitt, dressed in a purple sequin dress, appeared and stepped into the stage light.

I heard applause and shouts of praise, yet I was alone in the audience.

Emo spoke, "Thank you. Thank you for coming. I know my dad better now than I knew him when he was alive. I can talk to him in a way I couldn't before. And now when I have questions, in the quiet, he is honest with me. You can think whatever you would like about that." Emo walked over to the horse and guided it off stage. In a flash of bright light, Leonard Pruitt appeared in golden-white glory, center stage.

"Hello, Honey. How are you, my friend?" The familiar cantor of his South African voice sent chills all over my body.

I looked around the auditorium, and then a whisper escaped me. "*Leonard?*"

He smiled and his beauty sucked the air from me. And yet I felt peaceably breathless, not panicked. "Leonard!" I yelped. "I am so sorry. *I am so, so sorry.*" Tears came and although I knew I was dreaming and need only sit up to break free from all of this, I didn't want to leave.

"Oh, friend," he purred. "This is not on you. I'm okay. I want you to be okay."

"Why? Why do you care what becomes of me?"

"I care about love. Remember what I wrote? *Violence is an aggressive and selfish energy. It rudely interrupts the energy of peace with its demand to be served, to meet with what it wants.*"

I nodded.

Instantly, Leonard was in the seat next to me. I could see him, but more, I could smell his cologne. Somewhere in the background, I could hear myself saying, *It's just a dream.* But I wanted more of this, more of this feeling.

Leonard continued, "Love is all that matters. In life, we get to live and love in a body. It's such a privilege, Honey. The body allows us to taste, feel, and experience life. And the body is subject to illness and decay, death. But that ending is just a discarding of this body. Violence can do that. But we can also destroy ourselves by focusing on hate instead of being our true selves: *love*."

Suddenly he was back on the stage. "Look up from the prep table, chef. Bake a cake and then eat it. Write a novel and then read it yourself. Read it one million times and make the ending better and better each time. Forgive. And give everyone else a break, friend. It matters. That is what matters, not the perfection. Not the presentation. Just the love."

He disappeared and my eyes flew open.

Forgive? Forgive who? I immediately decided that it was just a stupid dream. But the blue lock box tickled my bandaged brain. If Mom has a love nest on West Park Avenue, and Dad has a key, *he knew*. And if Dad knew about the affair, their whole song and dance, the love story they modeled in the kitchen with love pats and waltzes was a lie.

Dad lied.

Mother lied.

Something I would have sworn neither of them would ever do.

But the fury?

I know that beast. And it is not my father. He may be connected to Leonard's death, but I refused to believe he was capable of the violence I met with in the garage.

There was no getting comfortable in the twin canopy bed. The cuff around my neck kept my head tilted just enough that my bruised sinuses were slammed shut. With no interest in lying in the dark, pondering deep, repetitive thoughts all night, I convinced myself to sit up. The quiet made me think louder. Which sounds crazy. Or at least, I thought so, until my thoughts grew so loud, they sounded like a scream. So, I achingly decided to get up and find something to eat.

And that is when I noticed, *I'm hungry*. Really hungry.

I put Mary Shelley to task as I recoiled at my Frankenstein's monster-like posture, casting gruesome silhouettes through the shadowy house. The dim streetlamps barely illuminated my path to the kitchen. Suddenly, I was so hungry and so ready to eat...something? Anything? But as I limped down the hall, I nearly face-planted as my trauma boot caught on the rug.

Stumbling, I clutched the wall, bracing myself and whimper-howling in pain. *Damn it!* The physical pain—miserable though it was—paled in comparison to my helpless fragility. My stumble must have alarmed Axel. Light from the guest room spilled under the closed door, and I heard the man's bare feet paddle across the hardwoods.

Creaaak. The heavy door cracked open, illuminating the narrow hall, and a sleepy-faced, bare-chested Axel peered out.

"Honey?"

I held my hand up, shushing him, whispering, "I'm starving!"

A smile spread across Axel's handsome face. He scratched his nose twice with his thumb and said, "Girl, I gotch you."

There was nowhere for me to sit comfortably in the kitchen. I hardly put up a protest as Axel, now comfortably dressed in gray sweats and a faded Hard Rock t-shirt, tucked me in on the den sofa. He lay the remote in my hand and dimmed the lights. And then he whispered over his shoulder, "Be back in a few with a feast."

My arm, as limp as a grossly overcooked noodle, couldn't lift the remote high enough to catch the television's sensor.

"That's brilliant, Honey. Too feeble to watch TV. Bravo," I spoke into the quiet, and then jerked in surprise as Bo's voice cracked the silence.

"Talking to yourself is a sure-as-shit-fire way to end up in a looney bin." Bo, dressed in flannel pajama bottoms and a familiar, worn, navy-blue cotton bathrobe, moseyed into the den with rather cautious steps. My stomach lurched as I recognized what he was wearing.

Dad's bathrobe.

IN LIEU OF EATING

I kept my voice steady, slightly jovial. "Hey, nephew."

Bo fell into the recliner, dropping his face in his hands. "What the hell, Aunt Honey?" he moaned. "I can't sleep. Who would do this to you? *What is happening to our family?*"

I didn't answer, remaining silent for who knows how long. Finally, I cleared my throat and said, "We are evolving. We are learning, Bo. We're still a family. And we are thriving." Bo lifted his head, eyes serious. The dim light cast shadows on his brow. In that moment, he looked so beautiful and grown up, I thought my heart might burst. I forced my brain to quelch a sudden desire to blurt out, *Don't grow up, Baby Bo!*

But then he spoke, his voice a mysterious combination of sadness and hope. "Aunt Honey.... I swear to God, *I smell bacon.*"

I'm not sure how Axel operated in our family for ten years and missed the memo on the Honeycutts and bacon. But as the smell of crispy pork filled the rooms—at 2 a.m.—everyone in the house: Mother, Marcella, Bo, Davy, Axel appeared, and we helped ourselves to mounds of bacon, hatch chili and cheddar cheese omelets, and bagels and cream cheese, picnic-style in the den. Davy hardly noticed how battered I was, being fully distracted by food and up past bedtime. Axel and Mother dashed back and forth as, at last count, I think a total of five pounds of bacon were delivered to us in the den, hot off the griddle.

Absolutely everything tasted divine.

It felt nearly strange to delight in flavors and textures again. Granted, the bacon had been cured in my restaurant—my signature recipe. But it tasted so much better than I remembered. The bite of cracked pepper was cooled with the sweetness of hickory smoke and traces of trademarked honey glaze. I felt guilty as I consumed helping after helping of crispy pork and fluffy, spicy, cheesy eggs. But as my thoughts drifted between Dad's situation and the feast and family gathered around me,

I decided with great intent...to live. I salted another bite, noticing how the flavors exploded on my tongue. I spread thick, whipped cream cheese on a chewy bagel, mixing some sweet bites with my "famous" huckleberry jam and others with savory tomato relish and freshly sliced jalapeño.

I noticed my family. Davy kept us in stitches, spinning tales full of all the things he planned to do when he grew up. His primary goal: to become the operator of a roller coaster with a traveling circus. Axel told us a story about his first job at a carnival, where he ran the cotton candy machine at the concession stand. Davy's eyes grew wide with envy and awe. His little voice begged, "Did you get free cotton candy?"

Axel said, "I got a discount, but I licked my fingers quite a bit."

Davy piped in, "Dude! That sounds awesome!"

My throat ached from laughing; my cheeks, bruised from the beating, felt comfortably tired from smiling. Finally, with the feeding hour over and our bellies full, the room quieted, flooded now with only the light from the television. A serene setting: Mother rocking in her rocking chair, eyes shut, brow released. With a kind of sudden revelation, I noticed that Mother seemed okay, at least at that moment, and it warmed me, a swell of appreciation blooming for her. I didn't consider the affair, although...seriously? No, I still didn't believe it. But if love was all that mattered, I wanted to know more about this woman I call Mom.

Axel sat in the window seat, leaning back, relaxed, a toothpick in his mouth. He stared out at our quiet street, and I wondered if he was feeling homesick for moments like this, loved ones with full guts in good company. Davy was curled at my feet, his "blankie" and warm body welcomed weight on my sore foot. With his stuffed elephant tucked under his chin, he moved every so often in reaction to the television screen. Marcella was balled up in an Afghan, lanky limbs edging off both ends of the loveseat.

Then my eyes fell on Bo—and froze there, hypnotized. As Bruce Willis battled not to die hard, and cinematic violence toyed with the ambiance, I stared. Marcella's face was out of view, turned toward the television, but one battered arm hung off the edge of the loveseat, dangling down—right to where Bo lay beneath her on the floor.

Bo was sprawled out, one arm behind his head. Dad's navy-blue robe hung open, allowing the television light to illuminate his skinny man-boy chest, accentuating with an eerie glow the few red hairs just beginning to peep out. But his other arm was nonchalantly, lightly swatting Marcella's hand, then grabbing it as if they were thumb-wrestling. They played this little game for a while, locking fingers like flirting teenagers and then quickly retaliating with pinches and grabs. In a kind of awe, I watched my sister, Bo's mother, her long fingers playing with her son's clumsy paws, her slim belly rising and falling with contentment and an occasional giggle.

I noticed. And then I realized something horrible. I would have scolded her for this moment, would have shamed and even accused her. *She plays footsy with her son in lieu of parenting.*

Mother's rocker squeaked as she shifted in her seat and our eyes met. I flicked my eyes back to Marcella and Bo; Mother followed my cue and then smiled. Seconds later, she lay her head back and seemed to drift off, a gentle grin illuminating her exquisite face. I wasn't mad at her, but I was curious, still watching as her face abruptly morphed, and she looked pained. I tried to imagine this woman, I thought I knew, her face beaming as she had twirled about the kitchen with my dad, how that bond between them could have been a lie. How so much of my life seemed that way—just lies. But not because of her, but because of all I had missed.

PALATE CLEANSE

People's parents break up, and yes, that sucks. But given the choice between separating holidays and awkward family get-togethers, I think the latter would have been my preference.

But no. This is more destructive. Maybe I blocked it, just didn't really want to know. Maybe it was obvious, and I hid in my kitchen so I wouldn't ever have to think less of her or me.

No longer hypnotized by the loving interplay between Bo and Marcella, I now sat entranced by my mother. The television light danced in hues of vibrant green, berry, and citrus on her now-pinched face. My eyes welled, and my fingers tingled at the thought of her soft yet calloused touch, felt by me so many times when I needed it throughout the years. The strength of her fingers, the command they demanded as they waltzed about the wood strings on her violin.

I had paid attention to her talent as a musician and mother. I swear, I had. Suddenly, Mother's brow furrowed, and she twitched a bit as if deep in a nightmare. Abruptly, she sat up and looked about wildly. Patting her cheeks, she adjusted herself and closed her eyes forcefully tight. A tear escaped her eyelashes on one side of her face. I watched its journey downward, finally dropping onto her jade-colored collar pajamas. She clutched the Afghan and rocked a little.

I could no longer watch her suffer. Though cowardice seemed preferable to confronting the truth, I couldn't take any more of this. Desperate, I wanted to stand and approach her, take her hand, and ask gently, *Who are you broken for, Mother? What haunts you? Is it true? Did you love Leonard Pruitt?*

I tightened the grip on my mind and began mentally peeling apples and reciting the recipe for my apple cobbler backward and forward in lieu of considering the womanhood of my mother.

IN LIEU OF EATING

I don't want her to suffer. I didn't want any family of mine to go through such anguish. I just wanted to take care of these people. And feed them bacon.

This is love. I felt every bit of the yellow light consuming me, but now, I was awake. My ears buzzed so much that I poked one earlobe with a sprained finger, as if to stop the ringing by flipping a mental switch. Which is the last thing I remember right before I dozed off. My last cognitive thought: *I wish Dad was here. He would want more of this, more of this love, more everything… in lieu of violence.*

Second Main Course

When I woke the next morning on the den sofa, everyone was gone. I could hear Mother and Axel bustling about in the kitchen. It felt late in the morning, though my eyes were too tired to read the numbers on the grandfather clock. My glasses were nowhere I could see. I yawned and stretched, both of which hurt. Rest, though, had become my friend since the attack, some of it drug-induced, and much of it a soothing lullaby of gratitude. I thought about, while lying on my back, stretched out on my parents' high-priced designer sofa, dressed in opulent pajamas, what a brat I had been. Wealth, opportunity, love… It was there, and I hadn't recognized it until it started slipping away. How silly, to have laid claim to some grand, brash uniqueness. A cleverly sweet nickname draped over a sour, spoiled bitch. I wanted to run even further from the person I had been before I experienced the trauma necessary to finally notice.

I groaned a bit, the pain subsiding but still on the periphery of my attention, and then rolled onto my side.

"Good morning, Honey." Axel entered the room and then stopped, his cup to his lips in mid-sip. "Oh! Let me go put down my coffee."

"No, no. Don't." I adjusted myself on the sofa. "It doesn't bother me as much. I'm considering having a cup myself. Besides, I can barely smell."

"Well, your sinuses are probably swollen."

"I hadn't noticed so much, except when I'm lying down." We sat in the awkwardness of rejected kisses and copious fried pork consumption.

"Any news?" I finally asked.

"Uh…" Axel cleared his throat. "Yeah. Lance was right. Your dad is in protective solitary custody."

"Do they know why?" I begged.

"We didn't get into it. Lance is coming here in an hour with an investigator on the case. A…uh…" Axel thought for a minute and then pulled a piece of paper from his jacket pocket and read. "A guy named Detective Ryan Cassum."

I began to get up, wanting to look somewhat human, considering all that was unfolding. "Can you help me get to my room so I can get ready?"

"Yeah." Axel moved to my side. "But, Clara, aren't you going to ask your mother about the penthouse? The affair? They'll be here in an hour. I think you need to talk to your mom before you talk to anyone."

"I don't want to tell the detective or Lance anything."

"What?"

"I don't want to tell them. Not yet." I stood impatiently, determined to get to my room.

Axel moved, grabbing an elbow. "This is a mistake, Clara."

"Maybe," I agreed. "But this is the first time I have anything tangible to go on. I am not giving it away for it to rot in some evidence room. No," I said. "I am done waiting for things to unfold. As far as anyone but you, me, and Marcella know, we cannot figure out what the combination is for. And for now, I am pretending I never heard the words *Mom and Leonard Pruitt were lovers.*"

SECOND MAIN COURSE

"How will you get Marcella to agree to that?" he asked as we made our way down the hall.

"Oh, she will love this. She aspired to be Daphne on *Scooby-Doo*." Axel huffed.

"What?" I asked.

"You and Marcella crime-solving." He deepened his voice theatrically as he rumbled out, *"Ru-Roh, Shaggy."*

Marcella was in our room, primping. She looked better. I had to inquire, "You have a different Gucci sling on?" I appraised her pointedly. "Did you have a collection of designer first-aid supplies in reserve in case an unexpected injury collides with your social calendar?"

"Yes?" she answered as if it was a stupid question. "Of course…?"

I would have laughed, but she was serious.

"Can you help me change?" I requested. "Lance Vega and a detective are coming to speak to us."

"Yeah," she said flatly, moving to the wardrobe, where Mother had moved several comfy tops and stretchy pants for me.

"Eeech." Marcella made a face.

"What?"

"Well, there's not much to choose from." She giggled. "Wait. *These are your clothes.* Like your current wardrobe. Ugh. Sorry, I don't think I can help you." She smirked at me over her shoulder.

"You have on ripped blue jeans and a Kermit the Frog t-shirt," I pointed out. *"From high school."*

"I know!" she squeaked. "Can you believe I still fit in these?"

I bit down the smart remark, *A good plastic surgeon and your daddy's checkbook can work miracles*, instead replying, "Marcella, please just get me those army-green, cropped palazzo pants and that peasant blouse with the yellow floral print."

Marcella complied and helped me dress and adjust my hair around the bandage I was terrified to look under.

"Let me put a little concealer on that cheek," Marcella clucked. "It will make you feel less victimized."

I snort-laughed. "Yes, a good facial is balm to the soul to assault victims everywhere."

"Oh, shut up." Marcella guided me to the vanity stool. I sat and she began to tinker with my hair and makeup.

"Marcella, I need you to not say anything else about Mother and Leonard. Especially to the lawyers and the police."

Marcella's reflection revealed her slight pout, but she playfully and gently twisted and sprayed each of my curls individually. "I haven't so far. I don't think it has anything to do with this. Like, I don't think that is why Dad killed Leonard."

My insides were screaming, but at this point, it didn't matter. "Okay, Sherlock. What do you think happened?"

Marcella considered my face and then said, "Turn around so I can get your nose and chin."

I obliged.

"Close your eyes," she further instructed.

"Marcella, I don't need eye shadow. Just tell me what you think."

"You're right, you don't need eye shadow. You need a good waxing. Clara, why would you let your eyebrows go like this? Have you given up completely?"

Which is when I lost it. "Marcella!"

"Fine." She strolled to her bed and flopped down. She picked up a tin box off the nightstand and began sifting through the contents. "I think that Dad's mafia connections finally caught up with him and they set him up. You know, framed him?"

SECOND MAIN COURSE

I just stared at her. Like, for an unreasonable amount of time. Finally, Marcella stared back and asked, "Are you having a seizure?"

"What?" I sputtered. "Mafia connections? Dad is an accountant! A restaurant business manager!"

Marcella let out a belly laugh. "Yeah. For the mafia." She casually looked at her nails. "Clara, I am your sister. You may not like me much, but you don't have to pretend. Dad is in prison. Gig's up. Don't tell me you didn't know."

My mouth was dry. I felt increasingly dizzy. I whispered, "I didn't know."

I stared at myself in the mirror. Surprisingly, there were no tears. The well had dried up. Finally, I was over any illusion that my dad had been involved in some unreasonable mishap of mistaken identity. I felt angry, though it was a different anger than what had caged me for so long. I wanted answers.

"I feel tired," I finally admitted.

"Well, that's to be expected," Marcella volleyed.

"No, tired of not knowing what is going on."

"Well, oblivion is your specialty," she teased.

"It's not funny, Marcella," I said flatly. "I built my life around the restaurant and working with Dad. I feel like, all this time, I have been a victim of a Ponzi scheme or something. Like, I don't even know who Mother and Dad are. And I can't bring myself to find out."

"Oh, good grief, Honey." She waved her hand at me. "You really are being over the top."

I stared at my reflection, well past disbelief when it came to the stuff Marcella always said, but at this point, I also didn't feel like being stomped on anymore.

"You suck, Marcella."

She stopped tinkering and looked at me with real shock. Before she could counter, I continued, "No, really. Can't you for just a moment consider what I am saying? I got my ass beaten within an inch of my life, which is obviously in connection with *a murder!* A murder our dad is in prison for! And *I am* being over the top in my questions?"

Marcella just shrugged. "I mean, it has been nearly a year. I guess… Yeah, it is weird that things don't seem to be dying down."

Exasperated, I changed course. "What do you know about Emo Pruitt?'"

Marcella, still sifting through the box, occasionally holding up lone earrings and opening old notes, said, "We were at NYU together. Since then, socially, I have been one of her 'starving artists,' so I have performed at Purple. I donate my take to the Center for Contemporary Arts. A lot of artists who don't need the mon—"

I cut her off. "No, I mean, does Emo know about Mother and Leonard—if it's true?"

Marcella shrugged. "I don't know. It's not something you bring up backstage. 'Hey! Did you know my mom and your dad are having a scandalous affair?'" She cocked her head slightly. "Why?"

"I ran into her the other day before the attack in the garage. She said that she doesn't believe that Leonard wrote the review of my restaurant. That someone else wrote it."

Marcella snorted. "Well, Dad probably wrote it."

Exasperated, I asked, "How would he have done that and gotten it published? You know what? *Never mind.* I will investigate it myself. I just thought *maybe* you might be of some help."

"I am of help. If you hadn't noticed, *you aren't dead.*"

"Yes," I agreed. "We aren't going to get past you saving my life. Thank you."

Marcella grinned mischievously. "You're welcome!"

I exhaled and continued. "I don't know, I felt a connection with Emo. She intrigued me. And I don't want to overstep, but I am thinking

SECOND MAIN COURSE

of reaching out to her. Tell her what happened in the garage and ask her about the penthouse. I hate to sound like some freaky mystic. But she seems... *familiar*. You know?"

"No," Marcella said flatly. "I have no idea what you mean."

Interesting how someone can save a life with a designer satin pump, risking their very own body, and not be able to decipher even a twinge of thoughtful contemplation. I inhaled jagged irritation. "Lord God, Marcella! I feel like I know her! As in a cosmic connection?"

"Oh, Honey, you really should steer clear of a lesbian relationship. With your bone structure and stature, you'll always pick up the check. It's a man's world, sis."

At this point, I felt an ungodly need to beat Marcella with my shoe. But I was too tired. "You're too stupid for me to spend much more time with."

Marcella huffed. "You know, you could take a beat and not try to be so brutal, *Honey*."

There was a catch in my throat as I mumbled my folly. "Okay, *I'm sorry*. Now you apologize for the bone structure jab."

Marcella looked at me, legitimate pity spread across her battered face. "Oh, baby. That was a valid directive. I wasn't being passive. I'm sorry you're built like Daddy too." She gave me a sympathetic pout and then began grooming her fat lips with some 1990s Bonne Bell Watermelon Lip Smacker lip balm from the nightstand drawer.

Defeated by my conflicting gratitude for Marcella's bravery and my desperate desire to watch her be disemboweled by werewolves, I mentally talked myself off the cliff. *She's your sister. She saved your life. She's as sensitive as a wet mop. But she's still your sister.*

I changed the subject. "Marcella?"

"Hmm?" She continued to mess with mementos from the past. But before I could speak, she said, "Come to think of it, she wouldn't be interested. Emo isn't a lesbian. That girl loves men and men love her. You will be hard-pressed to seduce her."

Now, rage is all I could muster. "I really do hate you."

She laughed. "No, you don't."

"Yes! I do!" I yelped. "Who says something like that? First of all, I am not a lesbian! I'm not anything. I am just…" I growled, "*Ugh!* You are infuriating! And what if I was a lesbian? That's not a joke! I am saying, I felt a connection with her in the loss, and that maybe she could help us get Dad out and get our lives back!"

Marcella stood, setting the box on the nightstand. "What life do you want back, Clara? The one where you have no idea what's going on right under your nose? Or the one where you judge all of us on *your* scale of morality?"

"No!" I snapped. "But they are our parents. Don't you want them to be okay?"

"Of course, I want them to be okay!" Marcella bit back. "But life happens. This could have been any number of tragedies, but you can't go back and fix *their* mistakes to make *your* life okay."

"I didn't know they had any mistakes." I softened my tone. "I thought they were the gauge for my perfection."

Marcella rolled her eyes. "Please, Honey, if we were innately programmed to have babies and live in Staten Island, making brownies for the PTA bake sale, Mom and Dad wouldn't be raising my sons. Humans are the worst kinds of parents. We're really the only species capable of selfishness. You ever see a bear leave her cub to go clubbing? Parenting for animals is innate. Parenting for humans is subjective."

I didn't say anything. I'm not a parent. But what Marcella said made sense. She continued, "Emo and her dad were companions. Like, I get that. But Honey, Leonard was getting something else on the side, and not to tell tales, but Emo is not hard up for suitors."

I nodded. "That is what I meant. I think she'd understand what I am going through."

Marcella shook her head. "You're comparing apples and oranges! You only hung out with Dad and cooked for the last however many years, content to ignore every other human bodily need or desire unless Axel lied to you and said, *"Hey, Honey, I got stood up. Want my extra ticket?"* She mocked Axel's accent perfectly, which made me giggle. That didn't stop her rant, though. "Bravo! That worked great for you! But everyone has a life outside of yours, Honey. Including Dad. Didn't you notice that he went to the club? Played tennis? Had season tickets to… *everything?* You've created this fantasy world where everyone had their assignments. It just caught up to you."

A tear escaped my eye as Marcella continued her scolding. "We are a family, but we're also individuals. Just because you were content to be in the kitchen, hanging out with Daddy, planning your next big win, doesn't mean that was all Mom and Dad needed." She lifted her breast, adjusting her boobs so they stood at attention around the sling, morphing Kermit into an exaggerated startled expression. "Besides, there is no going back, now that you know what you know. Which begs the question: What are you going to do to fix *your* life, Honey? They are grown-ass adults, and so are you."

She stood at the door, awaiting my response.

After a few minutes, I managed one. "I don't know. Everything I thought I knew seems wrong now. I have no idea how to start over or create something new."

"Well, no one can do it but you, *obviously.* And I wasn't making fun of you. I miss you. We were friends once." Her eyes changed. I almost thought I saw them moisten just a little. "Remember? When I say stuff about you like that, maybe part of it is ugly. Like, to make myself feel empowered. I can own that." She shuffled her feet and nodded. "But I don't think that's how it is with you. I think, no, I *believe* teasing you is the only way to have anything with you." She smiled, and there was no joy in it. "It's all we have now."

"What does that mean?"

"I don't know anything about you anymore." She sniffled. "Before Dad went… Before this mess, you cut all of us out. Except Dad."

"He's my friend."

"Is he?" Marcella volleyed. "Wouldn't a friend have been honest with you about his connections to criminal activity or admitted that his marriage was a joke?"

"Don't say that!"

"Fine," she spat. "Maybe I'm wrong. But look at you. Look at yourself! What makes you think *you're* right?"

And then she spun around and shut the door.

Just as I had when Axel had given me that tongue-lashing back in the garage, I just sat there silently. That was a lame exit, and I do hate her. Mostly. I looked at my reflection. Slightly smiling at the beauty mark Marcella had highlighted next to my busted lips. I pulled out a tissue and rubbed the mark off. I didn't hate her, honestly. Marcella was funny in a sick and twisted way. And she was right. I do have to rebuild my life.

Right after I figured out what the hell my old life was all about.

———

In the formal living room, Axel, Marcella, and I sat on the sofa while Lance and my mother sat across from us on the adjacent sofa. I sat there quietly, trying to recall the last time I sat in this room, mostly just passing by it in the past on my way out the front door. I never took much time to consider why I didn't just stop in this room, spend any time in it. It always felt too fancy for us. I preferred the coziness of the den or the vibrant, white kitchen with pops of exposed brick and blown glass, with its cobalt-blue light fixtures. The window to the street allowed the late-morning sun through, prohibiting me from seeing my mother's face or her expressions, though I knew this meeting had to be difficult for her. Lance introduced Detective Ryan Cassum, who reminded me of a game show host far more than anything else. Lanky and slick, with jet-black, overly dyed Elvis hair, he kept on display an enormous set of white teeth that overshadowed the rest of his face.

His accent was thick with Brooklyn slang, and he would inadvertently slightly bow and put his hand over his heart whenever he spoke to my mother. Which was…weird? Who did he think she was? Who did I think she was? *She's not royalty! She may or not be an adulterous monster! Who cheats on dads and makes them killers!*

Codeine, I thought. I couldn't concentrate. I felt lightheaded and itchy. The painkillers, I surmised, were making everything harder. Terrified that I might start yelping accusations and ruining lives in the process, I interrupted whatever information that had just passed without my knowledge by asking, "Could we close the drapes?"

I cleared my throat after everyone glanced my way. "Um, I'm sorry. The sun." I pointed at the window. "It's hurting my head, and I can't concentrate." Someone dashed to accommodate me, and then Axel leaned in and whispered, "Are you okay?"

I nodded.

The detective then continued, "As I was saying, we have identified the man who attacked you, Ms. Honeycutt, as Lorenzo Alioto Jr. On the streets, he is known by his nickname, 'Low.'" I looked about the room, seeing the reality of the situation crash over us in tsunami waves. As Detective Cassum continued, "Which is of great relevance because, as anyone who reads a newspaper knows, 'Low' is the youngest son of Mob boss, Lorenzo Alito Senior."

Lance chimed in, "We do not know what this has to do with Tom, but we suspect the cases are connected."

Cassum continued, "And while your father's case is not our priority at this moment, he has been advised of the attack on you and, as you know, is under protective custody."

"Prison isn't protective enough?" Marcella quizzed, now just a hair shy of being fully caught up to the dire situation.

Cassum spoke again. "This is a dangerous situation, and Alito's reach is growing, though he's not connected to much violence. But he has a lot of favors out. We suspect he is a key player in a drug smuggling operation the feds are closing in on. But these guys all have people on the inside and, as you well know, people on the outside to take care of family business. Word on the street is, Alito's son, Low, is now missing. We hadn't identified him, and the media doesn't know he's dead or about the attack on you, Ms. Honeycutt. So, there was a delay in our investigation. Low's car was towed and impounded about a block from here the night he came after you. That was the delay in identifying the body. He didn't have any ID on him and, unbelievably, his prints weren't in the system. Once the car came through processing yesterday, we realized whose name we had to put on the toe tag. After that, we ran his license and fingerprints again, and this time, we found a partial match in connection with Leonard Pruitt's murder."

"What?" I squawked. "The man who attacked me is associated with Pruitt's death? But why us? This doesn't make any sense." I paused. "He's dead, so he won't be back! Right?"

"Ms. Honeycutt." Cassum bent until eye level with me. "You said someone sent Low to teach you a lesson. Now the Godfather's bouncing baby boy is in the morgue with a hole in his neck from your sister's Christian Louboutin stiletto."

Marcella interjected, "That wasn't the death blow! I got him down with the mace and a crowbar! I just stepped on his neck in the scuffle. I think I killed him with—"

Lance interrupted, "Marcella, stop."

Detective Cassum continued. "This is all very serious. Now, if you can remember anything, if you know anything else that might help us, we need you to tell us."

I looked past Detective Cassum at my mother. She looked pale and fidgety but didn't return my gaze. My eyes darted around the room; everyone was staring at me. Everyone that is, except Mom. She just kept looking up in a corner, no definable expression on her beautiful face. Even her posture was odd, her back and neck straight, her jaw tight. I kept my eyes on her .until I quietly said, "No. I don't know anything else." Mother's body relaxed, and I watched as she dropped her head further into her shame.

I looked Cassum straight in the eyes, who gazed back with something akin to skepticism, and snarled, "*I have no idea what is going on.*"

Cassum stood, eyeing all of us suspiciously. "Well, I can tell you that Mr. Pruitt's watch was found at a warehouse in Queens. That's where the partial match finally connected Mr. Pruitt to Low, but not until after Low was dead." He paused, again eyeing all of us. "Are you listening?" he barked out, startling us all into erect poses. And then he sucked on his back teeth, making a clicking noise. "Well, for now, this is what we've got. Most likely, Alito's guys tracked Low's last assignment—silencing *you*, Ms. Honeycutt. That, coupled with your family's involvement in the murder of Leonard Pruitt, should prove more than enough. We *are* going to put the pieces together." He put his hands on his hips, scowling at each of us in turn. Cassum exhaled, then capped his speech with, "In my line of work, normal, upper-crust New York families don't implode into the bowels of criminal associations overnight." He folded his arms, and I could feel Marcella's ribs jiggle. I could tell she was about to start laughing, and then I was going to start laughing, and then we were both going to be arrested.

Cassum stepped closer and stood over us, again moving his hands to his hips. "I think you two are part of the problem. You and your little friend *Emo?*"

Marcella stopped jiggling. "Emo? What would any of this have to do with Emo?"

The detective leaned in until his nose was just inches from hers. "I don't know, maybe you all got tired of waiting for an inheritance? Maybe you and Emo conspired to knock off your parents, and it's time to pay the toll?"

Marcella snort-laughed in his face.

Lance leaped in. "Detective, let's stick to the issue at hand, please." Lance shot Marcella and me a death glare. We bowed our heads shamefully.

Then I whispered, "This is like a movie."

Marcella peeped, "I know, right!"

Cassum began again. "We suspect Alito's people are watching the house now, so we need to get you moved."

Finally, my mother sprung to life, gasping out, "*The boys!*"

Lance consoled her, "Sylvie, it's okay. Bo and Davy have been taken to a temporary location."

Axel leaned toward my mother, looking apologetic. "Yeah, uh, Sylvie, when I took the boys to get donuts, Lance met me in the garage. They're safe, I promise. I just texted with Bo." Axel held up his phone.

Relief washed over my mother. She clutched her lean, long fingers to her chest, eyes sunken and skin pale, and whispered, "*les bébés n'ont pas besoin de souffrir plus.*"

"The babies need not suffer more," Marcella whispered in my ear. And I pinched her as hard as I could with sprained fingers, gritting through my teeth, "*I know French!*"

"*Ow!*" Marcella yelped, then pointed at me while staring up at Cassum. "Detective! She pinched me."

"Ladies." Cassum turned to us. "I don't have time for games. You have one hour to get your things together. We don't have a place for you yet. But we're working that out now. I will be in touch with some details in a—"

"I have a place," my mother whimpered.

Lance turned to her. "Sylvie, Alito will know all—"

"No. He won't know about this. No one does." She patted Lance's hands. "I have an apartment, a penthouse apartment. It is still in my family estate's name. It has a private elevator entrance. You can only get past the penthouse with a key. It will be safe, and we will be comfortable. It's in the same building as Emo Pruitt's apartment."

Detective Cassum narrowed a glare at my mother, looking concerned and confused for a moment, and then said, "Actually, we might be able to work with that. Ms. Pruitt hasn't been moved yet. Let me make some calls." He turned to Lance. "I'll be in touch." And he left.

Everyone but me darted about the house collecting things. I could have helped, but instead, I fell back on old nature. As I did in the garage, and as I did when Marcella spoke so many truths, I just sat there. Only this time, I was alone in a fancy room that no one ever sat in except for during police interrogations. I closed my eyes and chanted in my head, *Rewind, rewind, rewind.* The prompt had never worked before and wasn't working now, not that I really wanted it to. This time, I wanted time to slow down, to press pause and just have a minute to accurately put the pieces of my life back together.

"Clara?" My mother's voice beckoned me from my trance. "Clara, are you all right? Can I get you something?"

I huffed out, "The truth?"

IN LIEU OF EATING

Mother's facade of innocence and motherly concern dropped, and she drifted elegantly to the sofa beside me.

"Mr. Alito was at the restaurant opening, the soft opening *and* the grand opening." My voice shook as I recalled visiting Alito's table. "He was there, *with his son*, Low. Dad's *special* guests."

My mother nodded. "He helped your father win the bid on the 57th Street location. He, uh, he and your father play tennis. They've been friends for years."

My intestines cramped, and I felt hot and freezing in equal measure. And then horrifically stupid. I took some pride in my notion of being a shrewd businesswoman. That my grit and charm, and the outstanding menu, had swayed the owners of the 57th Street location to pick me. I knew my parents' money didn't hurt my chances. But by that point, I had my own money for the restaurant. Now I was learning that all that old knowledge, more bricks in the foundation of my adult life, was a lie too. My voice cracked, "Is everything a lie? Dad is tennis partners with a criminal? You and Leonard? Mother? I don't understand!"

She paused, taken a bit back, and then shook her head. "You were always so busy. I wondered if you ever even suspected." She nearly hummed as she spoke.

"No," I spat. "Apparently, I am the last one to know. And Dad knew?" I said it more than questioned it. "Don't answer!" I yelled, then tried to collect myself. "That combination…?"

She nodded, head hung heavy with what I assume was shame.

"It was a lock box at the warehouse in the West Village. And do you know what was in it?" I didn't let her answer. "A key and an address to a penthouse on West Park! *So, Dad did know!* What the hell, Mother? Who are you people?"

She sighed, patting down and smoothing her expensive, calico-printed lavender A-line skirt. Then she paused, long fingers at her waist as her eyes traveled down her starched white blouse. She adjusted a pearl button, then reached up to smooth and pat at her long, salt-and-pepper hair. Seeming unsatisfied with that simple grooming, she grabbed her hair at the base of her neck, twisted it up, and then casually pulled a shimmering hairpin from her pocket and secured the twist.

"Mother!" I yelled out, exasperated. "This isn't a television interview. No cameras in our face, no audience watching. Stop trying to look perfect. *I'm your daughter!* What in the hell is going on?"

She furrowed her brow. "Don't raise your voice at me, Clara Louise." She stood abruptly and walked over to the bar behind the grand piano. I watched her open the mini fridge, pull out a chilled glass, and fill it with something gold-colored from a crystal canter, not spilling a drop. She downed it in one graceful gulp, and I felt jealousy and nausea tussle. Beauty and grace… Ever calm and collected. These traits defined the woman even in her worst moments while there I sat, wrestling down hysterics.

After setting down the glass, she turned, walked to the piano, and tapped a key. Finally, my mother stood to face me, hands folded in front of her at her groin, a body language move of innocent-guilt.

"Yes." She nodded. "He knew. I…" She seemed to wither, shrinking into herself before falling into the chair a few steps to the left of me. "Your father knew that Leo, *eh-hmm,* Leonard and I were lovers…. We had been together for over nineteen years." She said it politely and then sniffled out a little whimper.

I jumped off the sofa, instantly regretting the quick movements, and then wobbled on my wounded leg, desperately trying to stay upright. "What? Are you freaking kidding me? Are you sure?"

She looked at me, her expression a combination of disbelief and concern. *"Am I sure I had an affair?"*

Recognizing the silliness in my phrasing, I corrected, "No…" I fell back on the couch, which was too fancy and firm to react kindly to the sudden impact of all my weight dropping onto it. "Are you sure…?" I sucked in air. "That's not the right question."

Mother removed a handkerchief from her pocket and dabbed at her nose. "There is no point in asking silly questions," she said sternly. "I did it. I did it and your father knew. I told him the moment I knew I was in love with Leonard."

That pulled me even further into my vortex of utter shock. Where the hell was I right now? What was this? This looked like my childhood home. Two classic brownstones turned into one enormous, beautiful, warm, and loving home. The only home on the block with a garage and carriage house. That is how I would have described my home to anyone who asked before the allegations started. Now, I have no idea where I am. "Mother," I whisper-gasped, "you don't love Dad?"

She sniffled. "I do love Tom. And Tom adores me. But he treated me as if I were a character in The Tom Honeycutt show."

My stomach lurched at the accusation…and the jarring revelation that followed. It was Marcella's precise accusation of me.

My mother continued, "We were friends. But he hadn't treated me as a… Well, basically after you were born, he never touched me."

"That's not true!" I howled. "You danced in the kitchen, and he'd spin you! And kiss!" I argued like a toddler.

My mother shook her head. "Oh, Clara, darling, when is the last time you had your hormones checked? You know, your thyroid gland can slow your metabolism and lower your sex drive."

"Mother!"

"I can explain some more once we have moved. You need to be willing to listen to me, Clara. I won't make excuses for my behavior. But your father was content to create an empire that far exceeded the one we already had. And he was fulfilled in being a father and grandfather. I wasn't ever his priority." Her voice faltered. "Our marriage was never a priority. We were roommates. And friends."

"Friends?! Friends don't cheat on each other."

"Really?" Mother looked at me, chin up, raising her eyebrow. "Do you have any friends?" She folded her arms. Smiling sadly, she went on, "Maybe it's not hormonal. Maybe it's genetic. Although, even your father had hobbies and companions, Clara." She raised an eyebrow at me, then cleared her throat. "I was lonely. I was honest with your father. He would make attempts at fitting me into his life, and I tried, I really did. Darling, I even took tennis lessons!"

"You did?" I asked, surprised at the idea of my elegant mother covered in sweat and diving across a tennis court to crack her racket against a fuzzy, dirty little green ball.

"Yes." Her voice less defeated now, she plowed on, "I wanted to be his wife. I wanted the waltzes and sweet words to be in private too. Not just part of Tom's habitual morning routine."

We sat in silence for a few moments. I could have gagged, but not in judgment of my mother. The very idea she had an affair was still beyond me *but for nineteen years?* That's not an affair, that is an ongoing event. The gag reflex was from the continual, despicable lies now catching up to the Honeycutts like starved wolves hunting a rabbit.

"Fine," I spat, angrier with myself than my mother. "Fine," I softened. "But, Mother, I need to understand what is going on."

She nodded and stood. "I know" was her whispered response as she crossed the room, stopping at the entrance, where I barely heard her say, "*Oui. Tout vient à l'esprit.*" Then she continued out of the living room.

Yes. It's all coming to a head. I exhaled, whispered it, and then said it again, this time in my dad's language. "Shit's 'bout to hit the fan."

IN LIEU OF EATING

I dreaded the next few discoveries I knew were heading my way like a freight train, and yet I craved them like great chocolate after a snot-slinging, PMS-induced breakdown.

Knowing the truth in lieu of knowing nothing had to be better than this... It just had to.

Cheese Course

It was hours later when we were escorted from the house by a pair of quiet men in suits, all following the commands of Cassum. Taking with us only a scant number of belongings, Axel, Mother, Marcella, and I were nudged out the back of the house, led into a van behind the garage, and then driven around the city for at least an hour, switching vans twice. Finally, we pulled into a gated underground garage. Detective Cassum arranged for a wheelchair for me, and Axel took charge of pushing me through a dozen halls and heavy metal doors before finally arriving in front of a shiny, black elevator door. Mother opened her bag, pulled out a key, and inserted it into a hole behind an etched, brass panel. Two young, uniformed officers nodded to Cassum as he instructed my mother to take us up.

As the doors closed, Cassum piped to the officers, "Let me know when the Honeycutt boys are here. I'll come down and get them."

Inside the elevator, Mother opened a brass panel above the elevator buttons, revealing a keyhole and a button that read "PH". She slowly inserted the key and pushed the button, and we began our ascent toward my mother and Leonard's secret love shack.

IN LIEU OF EATING

I could feel the detective's eyes on me, but as the elevator doors opened, all gazes swung toward the penthouse. Here, I thought I couldn't be any more shocked by the secrets unraveling in my world. Turns out, I was wrong. The penthouse boasted twenty-foot vaultings with floor-to-ceiling windows that exposed views of the city I had only seen from the Empire State Building observatory deck in the seventh grade. Shiny, white marble floors, pillars, and a statuary of cherubs and naked women lined the walls. The crown molding was delicately outlined with gold foil that accented the heavy, blood-red, velvet-and-gold embossed scrolling wallpaper. Dense, scarlet drapes hung long at intervals across the expansive room. There were huge palms in elaborate pots—at least twenty of them throughout the space. To the left stood a fountain with fat carp swimming beneath water lilies in the stone pond below the faucet. In the far-right corner of the open space, at the window, sat a grand piano grand enough to put the one sitting in our house to shame.

A tufted, hunter-green chaise lounge and a dark, serious-looking leather sofa completed the seating space, all of it neatly arranged on an elaborate blue-and-gold Persian rug. In the center of the room hung a brass and crystal chandelier that stretched at least five feet in diameter. The Byzantine light fixture dripped with large, twinkling stones and intricate curling loops.

We all stood in stunned silence until Mother interrupted our awe. "This is just the entry room. To the right are the guest bedrooms, an office, and a den. To the left is my…" She trailed off. "I will sleep in the main room behind the kitchen. Davy can stay with me. Detective?" She turned to Cassum. "If you don't mind, my family is eager to get settled."

Detective Cassum nodded. "My guys have done a sweep of the apartment. You can have some time this afternoon and evening to get settled. I'll be back first thing in the morning to speak with you individually." He stopped and took a step toward my mother. "I'll be starting with you, Mrs. Honeycutt."

Mother faced the detective with a limp expression, face once again void of anything readable. And then he did that crazy bow thing that continues to confuse me.

"That will be fine, Mr. Cassum."

Detective Cassum and my mother kept up the odd staring contest for a few seconds longer, and then the detective sucked on his back teeth, making that clicking noise, then shook his head disapprovingly and left. Mother shifted into mom mode and began directing Axel to take bags to different rooms of her choosing. I moved to the sitting area and sank onto the chaise lounge. I lay there motionless, staring at the city I thought was my home. But it looked sinister and frightening now.

Marcella, not one to be tasked with any kind of bag delivery, sat down on the piano bench. "Wait until you get a load of the bedrooms."

I tried to zone back in. "Huh?"

"The bedrooms? And the den? I couldn't find the office. Must be a hidden panel or something," she muttered. "Most everything was covered in white sheets. Mom and I pulled them all off. She said she hasn't been here in several months, except to water plants. She closed it up after—"

"Do I have my own room?"

Marcella grimaced. "Well, it is a huge place. But no. There is a room with two queen-size beds for you and me. And then Axel and Bo will sleep in the room on a set of twin beds. We have to share a bathroom with them. Then there is another room with a king-size bed and an ensuite. I guess Emo will stay in there."

I felt a wave of relief. I wanted privacy, but I didn't want to be alone.

Marcella continued to chatter, "Wait until you see the den!"

A random tear popped out of my eye. I stared at the little side table next to the couch. A book lay open, with a pair of men's readers holding the spot. Next to the book sat a notepad and pencil with some cursive scribble, I couldn't make out. But it was not my mother's tidy, loopy writing. My gut lurched and another tear tumbled out. He was here. And not just on a whim. They had a life here. My mother and Leonard had led an entirely separate existence in this penthouse.

Marcella snapped her fingers. "Honey, don't fall apart on me."

I sniffled. "I just can't believe any of this. What is this place?"

Marcella snorted. "It looks like a cross between a French museum and a brothel. Kind of reminds me of that Casino in Vegas…?" She thought for a moment, tapping her finger on her chin.

"Caesar's Palace?" I offered helpfully.

"No." She thought longer. "I can't remember the name."

I inhaled a ragged, painful breath and ignored her.

"Come on, Honey!" Marcella said playfully. "Let's go see the den. I think it will make you feel a little better."

I doubted that, but I agreed and hobbled down the lacey, red-and-gold embossed hallway to an enormous window-lined room. The ceiling was lower, and despite the windows, the room felt dark. A bar lined one wall. It was very obviously an antique, sporting a large, aged mirror and dozens of exotic liquor bottles lining the shelves. Three beer spouts gleamed, and shelves that held heavy crystal wine glasses and a variety of mugs and shot glasses lined the back. The bar had a brass foot pole and lofty, black leather and cherry-wood barstools. A billiard table sat in the corner by a section of windows. My eyes moved to the sunken theater area with a big screen TV that took up the entire wall.

I wanted to be furious. My mother's extracurricular love life included not just lies and scandal but top-of-the-line luxuries. Yet the wall adjacent to the television lulled me into a passive, nearly spiritual trance. A poster from Marcella's show had been framed on the wall, suspended in a soft glow by the museum light that hung over it, illuminating Marcella dressed in a vibrant, cobalt-blue-sequined dress, the white horse standing next to her. In pink neon scroll, it read, *One Cobalt Blue Shot of Tequila. Marcella Monet. One night only!*

My eyes drifted to the poster next to it and what it revealed: my dad and me standing in front of my first restaurant. And next to that, with the same intentional care and consideration, was a poster announcing the grand opening of Emo's place, Purple.

Marcella stood next to me. "Cool, huh?"

"I guess," I mumbled.

"She's still our mother, Honey. This speaks to their relationship. They were proud of their children even in private." Marcella's eyes momentarily froze on her poster. She spoke again. "Besides Bo and Davy, that was the scariest thing I ever did…until now."

"What?"

"That show." She pointed to her poster.

I didn't say anything. That show still mystified me, as did my sister.

"When I sang that song, I just kept my eyes on Dad and Mother."

"*Song?*" The question escaped me, and I watched hurt creep over Marcella's face.

She swallowed hard and then put on a playful guise. "Wow, you must have zoned out real hard or hung out in the bathroom." She feigned superficial annoyance. "Yeah, I sang a song I wrote…while *naked* on stage."

"Oh! Yes, of course." I lied, remembering nothing about it. That's when I noticed a slim brass panel on the wall. I pointed a splinted finger at it. "What is that?"

Marcella pushed on it, and a door opened. She squeaked, "Oh, cool! It must be the office!" We stepped inside a room lined with bookshelves that all reached to the glass ceiling. Nothing but the blue skies above illuminated the room. The dark wood of the shelves carried to the molding and baseboards, where four cardboard boxes held books. Leonard's name marked the boxes, and there was dust on the empty shelves above. I walked the perimeter of the room, noticing the places where books seemed to have been removed.

Two overstuffed, navy chairs sat empty, each with matching ottomans. Between the chairs, an oiled brass lamp with a blown-glass lampshade, intentionally arranged on a twisted piece of wood that had been masterfully crafted into a table, stood there tastefully, though not in use. On the floor, a used dog bed sat with no visible owner, housing only a lime-green rubber chew toy.

"Look at this," Marcella called to me from behind a rustic desk that looked like the end table. I hobbled her way.

She pointed to the desktop monitor, and we stood and watched the screen saver roll out photos of our lives. Marcella holding Bo as a baby. Me speaking at a chef's convention. Davy playing soccer. Bo at a debate competition. Intermingled with Honeycutt pictures were shots of Emo, both as a young child and as the woman she had grown into.

"What the heck?" I murmured as picture after picture scrolled, rose, fell, and faded. Birthday parties, graduations, Christmases, none of them showing Leonard and my mother together, only the running record of how much they were apart. Marcella touched the mouse, and I pipped, "Don't!" Too late—the screen came to life; the desktop home screen revealed the intimate connection.

My mother and Leonard in a selfie on a rooftop, the New York sky behind them. Leonard's eyes closed, a peaceful smile on his lips. His nose nuzzling my mother's ear as if smelling her like a rose. My mother's face, forever immortalized in its contentment, decorated in shades of laughter and joy. Her dark hair with its slips of silver caught lifted over her shoulder in the wind as her dark eyes swam with delight. A lump rose in my throat as I stared at the still shot of bliss.

"Oh." My mother's voice alerted us. "You found the office."

"Mother?" I barely whimpered. "What is this place?"

My mother folded her arms. "Clara, it is exactly as it appears. I can't do this right now, but if you don't mind, I would rather no one be in here. I haven't had time to clear out some of Leonard's things."

Marcella jumped in. "So, let me show you our room, and then we can get our jammies on and watch movies." Mother motioned us out, closing the office behind her. And then she quickly walked around us back to the kitchen, her modest leather pumps clicking on the marble. I tried to keep up with Marcella, inquiring as I followed, "Do you know what's going on with Emo?"

Marcella nodded. "She just texted me. She will be up here at the same time as Bo and Davy. She's been told there may be a mafia connection to her dad's murder, and the concern is, she could be in danger. But she seemed oblivious about this place. So that'll be awkward!" Marcella giggled and proceeded to briefly and barely show me the other rooms, all of which looked dark, elaborate, and unused. Our room was very much like the French hotel rooms we would stay in while visiting Mother's extended family in France. Two matching, antique, rod iron beds and gaudy cherry wood nightstands—each with a brass lamp and matching embroidered lampshade—filled the space. The beds were tucked in with starched white sheets with heavily embroidered throw pillows atop them. Again, the walls were covered in velvety wallpaper, but in this room, it was blue and white Toile print.

"Our bathroom is here; it connects to a shower and Axel and Bo's room," Marcella explained. "Do you want a bath or anything? There's not a tub in this bathroom. But there is one in the other room. I can help you?"

"No," I said. "I can get cleaned up later. Really, I would love to have a few minutes to myself."

"Do you have your phone?"

"Yes."

"Okay." She touched my arm maternally. "I'm going to help Mom in the kitchen. She wanted to have food out when Emo and the boys get here. Text me if you need help. Okay?"

"Yeah, thanks."

She left and I locked every door in the room and sat down on the bed, opened my phone, and typed, "One Cobalt Blue Shot of Tequila" into the search bar. I scrolled through a couple of articles, clicked on a video, was forced to watch a Buick Enclave commercial, and then sat in awe as my sister began to sing acapella buck-naked.

I watched in blinding horror as I realized, I never even gave Marcella a chance. I didn't even remember this part of the show. I hadn't looked up from my self-induced haze. I had missed out on who my family was. *Who they are.*

The words spooled out across the bottom of the screen as Marcella semi-squawked the lyrics.

> *Spirit of story come now and rescue me.*
> *Set captives free, help us learn to believe.*
> *Something better, something more, in lieu of all we hate.*
> *Sing Spirit of Peace.*
> *Sing Spirit of Equality.*
> *Sing Spirit of Sight, sound, and love…*
> *Spirit of Story what was this place I stand*
> *Before hate*

CHEESE COURSE

Before war...
Spirit of story come now, expose me that I might remind
The world—who we are.
Without this flesh, I am as you are.
Spirit... write a new story.

A knock came at the door. My mother's voice startled me, and I closed my phone.

She spoke through the door. "Honey, Axel and an officer are bringing the boys and Emo up. I've set up a buffet of appetizers and snacks. Do you need anything?"

"No!" I barked and then softened my tone. Who was I to be so hateful? "No, Mother, I will be right there. Thank you."

It was several seconds before I heard her footsteps click away down the fancy marble hall. I steadied myself. Mentally promising myself, before I lay my head on a pillow, I would get all the answers I had been craving. The truth in lieu of lies.

Bo and Davy went straight for the big-screen TV. Bo had kept to his promise so far and hadn't caused a moment's trouble in nearly twenty-four hours, a personal record. Furthermore, he and Davy seemed happy, content, and far less traumatized than I would have expected. Emo seemed miffed. She was quiet but friendly, asking only to have some time alone in the room she'd been assigned. Kevin, the Irish Setter, seemed right at home in the luxury penthouse and greeted my mother like a long-lost friend, which made Emo seem even more disoriented. She quickly excused herself, dragging Kevin behind her.

When Emo and Kevin were tucked away in their room, and Axel and the boys were busy in the den, Mother, Marcella, and I sat at the kitchen bar, silent. I picked at the artichoke dip and drank a glass of cranberry juice, which needed some vodka but not nearly as much as I needed clarity. So, I downed it and pretended it was a cocktail.

"Mother, I feel like it's time for you to talk to us, don't you?"

She nodded, then stood, walked to the sink, and then put her plate down.

She turned and faced Marcella and me and spoke. "I know. I know you want and deserve answers." She politely cleared her throat. "It's 7:00 and I need to tend to Davy. "And…" She trailed off. "…I don't want to be interrupted. I want to tell you everything. If you'll excuse me, we will speak after he is asleep."

I was so sick of this, but I also knew that Davy would need to be settled before we would get much done.

"Fine," I spoke. "Marcella, I think we should probably check on Emo." Marcella helped me off the stool and down the hall to Emo's room. I could hear Axel and Bo playing pool. Emo's door was shut, and Marcella and I stood outside for several seconds before she whispered, "What if she doesn't want to talk to us?"

I shrugged and volleyed, "Well, we have to ask if she is okay or needs anything." The last word left my lips just as the door swung wide, and there Emo stood before us, Kevin at her side. She looked pissed. Gorgeously pissed.

"What in the hell is going on?" she asked flatly and then motioned us into the room. Emo's room was twice the size of Marcella's and my guest quarters and decorated in deep, rich greens and golds. An enormous, four-poster, cherry bed with a large impressionist-style painting of a lake and mountains hung above it. Two black, marble-topped nightstands, neatly styled on either side of the bed, held ornate Tiffany lamps that illuminated the room. The comforter on the bed looked to weigh as much as the mattress. It was a shimmery, satin taupe and scrolled with hand-stitched gold roses and knotty green leaves. A television perched on another wall above a fireplace with a seating area made up of a gold-colored couch and two matching wingback chairs. On the coffee table were three heavy, brass candlesticks ending in dark-green cylinder candles, far too flawlessly smooth to have ever been lit.

"Get in here," Emo demanded and we followed her inside to the sitting area.

She opened a large, ebony-stained armoire in the corner and said, "I found a bar. I think we all need a drink."

Somehow Marcella and Emo both started chatting about a local artist who was killed in a traffic accident while they mixed cosmos and poured nuts and pretzels into a bowl like this was all old hat to them.

Emo handed me a drink, and although I resolved not to take so much as a sip, the entire Cosmo was oscillating through my veins before Emo sat down.

She looked at me over the rim of her glass. "Well?"

"You may know as much as we do." I set my empty glass on the coffee table, and Marcella mindlessly picked it up and set it on a coaster. As if a ring on the coffee table was the priority right now.

Emo snapped, "Why don't you try me?"

I started with all I knew; Marcella added a few embellishments. "Basically, all we know right now is, our mother and your dad were lovers for the last nineteen years. This is their secret love nest," I finished.

Emo sat staring into nothing; despite her radiant, milk chocolate complexion, she looked pale.

She finally downed the rest of her Cosmo and asked, "So your dad killed him? And then sent in a fake review of the restaurant as a motive? Why wouldn't he just say the affair was the motive?"

IN LIEU OF EATING

Before I could stop the words, they spilled out in a shrill, defensive accusation, "Stop saying that! My dad is not capable of killing anyone!"

Emo narrowed her eyes at me. "God, Clara!" she snapped. "*Get over it!*"

I snapped back, "*Over it?* None of these people, our parents, are who we thought they were! But I promise you, my dad did not beat your dad into pulp and shoot him in the head!"

Emo's eyes flooded, and she stormed to the bar, poured two shots of something, and then stormed back to the chair where she had been sitting. Kevin stood, wagging his tail. She snapped her fingers and said, "Sit down and shut up, *Kevin!* You're obviously right in the middle of this mess, you lousy traitor. I ought to ship your butt to the breeder and tell her good riddance!" Kevin fearfully lay down, obviously hurt.

Emo took a deep, ragged breath. "I feel…" She closed her eyes. The woman, as stunningly beautiful as she was, was also what I would describe as emotionally stable, which I envied. She continued, "I feel like my whole life is a lie." She sniffled, untucking her pink camisole. Her narrow belly flashed, revealing a small tattoo that read, *Notice Love* in thick script. She reached into the pocket of her blue jeans and pulled out a folded piece of paper. She tossed it to Marcella, who unfolded the note and read it out loud.

"Sylvie, I will not be threatened or manipulated. It's over. We are too old for games. I will finish removing my things from the penthouse by the end of the week. The rest is done. Leave us alone. L

"Us?" I inquired.

"Well, he didn't mean me," Emo explained. "I can't get any more clueless. I did not know about him and your mother, and I certainly didn't know about this place. Dad had money, a lot of money. But the HOA on this building is $4,000 a month. What do you suppose this penthouse runs?"

CHEESE COURSE

Marcella took a sip of her Cosmo and said, "I think my parents own this building."

"We don't know that," I countered.

Marcella sipped and nodded, "The panel in the elevator said Romanoff Estates Inc."

"Mother's maiden name," I whispered.

"So, you two don't know anything either," Emo acknowledged with a twinge of contempt and then picked the remote up off the coffee table and started punching buttons. "If my dad weren't dead, I think I'd kill him."

Marcella boasted, "I know more than you two. I knew about Mom and Leonard for years."

I sighed. "Okay, how is that?"

"I saw it unfolding." Marcella snorted. "I still don't get that you never did. Honey, you didn't notice anything off with Mom and Dad? You never noticed her dressed differently or home late? Didn't you ever listen in on their conversations?"

"No." My ears were ringing, and I whispered under my breath, "I had no idea."

"Where did you get this?" Marcella waved the note Emo had found.

"It was in my dad's raincoat pocket." Emo sipped her Cosmo. "I finally started going through some of his things. So far, it is the only trace of evidence that I have found that they were having an affair."

Marcella and Emo began spouting what I consider outlandish theories until I interrupted.

"Emo, who is your mother?"

"What?"

"Who is your birthmother?" She and Marcella both just stared at me while I rattled off my outlandish hypothesis. "What if you are Sylvie's daughter? What if she is lying, and they have been together this whole time, and she gave you to Leonard, and she and my dad raised Marcella? Like, what if you two are twins?"

Marcella and Emo stared at me, blinking in confusion, and then burst out in heaving laughter.

Emo snorted and guffawed. "I'm pretty sure I was born of a poor soul on the streets of Cape Town, South Africa. The little I do know is that she blackmailed my dad—and his parents paid her off and then migrated to the United States. But I love your mind, Clara Honeycutt," she howled, holding her stomach in pained laughter. She and Marcella continued to belly-laugh and then began to sing, *"Let's get together, yeah, yeah, yeah… Why don't you and I combine? Let's get together, what do you say… ?"* while Marcella scrolled the big screen looking for the movie.

"We *have* to watch it!" Marcella cackled. "It's *The Parent Trap!*" she squealed and Emo said, "Let's watch the original first!"

"Stop laughing!" I yelped.

"Oh, Honey!" Emo waved her hand at me. "Lighten up."

"Lighten up!?" I barked. "How can you two laugh like this? Aren't you disgusted? Aren't you upset?"

Emo stood motioning to us in reference to another cocktail as she made her way to the bar again. We both nodded greedily. She mixed and spoke. "Life happens all at once and in episodes. If we don't laugh when we need to laugh, cry when we need to cry, we implode."

"Yeah," Marcella concurred. "Who's to say when it's okay to laugh or cry? Especially when you just pulled that rabbit out of your hat!" She snort-laughed and Emo started up again too. "Oh, my gosh! Is that not the worst storyline in the world!? Two people splitting up twins so they never have to see each other again!" She howled.

Marcella choked on her Cosmo. "I gave my kids away, but at least I told them!" And they cackled some more.

I sat soaking in the filth of my humiliation and watched the beautiful people having a glorious time at my expense, and then...I lost it. And screamed at the tops of my lungs until I couldn't breathe.

"*Aaaaaaaaaahhhh!*"

Which brought the party to a complete stop.

"What in the hell are you doing, Clara?" Marcella asked.

"Screaming," I explained. And then I opened my mouth and did it again.

Marcella pleaded, "*Stop it, Honey!*"

But Emo interjected, "No. Let her." So, I did it again. And again. And again.

And then panting in the relief of release, I wheezed, "I'm done."

Marcella looked completely mystified. "What was that?"

I couldn't speak. Mother came running, busting through the door without knocking, a look of horror on her face as she gulped, "*Hit... the... alarm!*" And Marcella rushed to explain.

Emo walked cautiously toward me and knelt in front of me.

She brushed a curl from my forehead and tucked it behind my ear. "It's okay, Sylvie. Honey just had something stuck in her throat. It needed to get out. It's okay now." She leaned her head gently against mine and whispered, "It's okay now."

I just sat. Marcella and Emo sedated my mother with a Cosmo, which was only fair.

Bo and Davy didn't stir, which was disturbing. Marcella was somehow coherent enough to ask, "Where is Axel? Didn't he hear that?"

"No." My mother shakily raised the glass to her lips. "He went to the gym on the twelfth floor."

The television was still on. I could hear cordial conversation in the room now, but I couldn't participate. I don't know how long I sat staring at the fifty-two-inch blue screen. But the words *The Parent Tra…* and a blinking cursor were burnt into my retina.

Emo was right; the screams were stuck in my throat. I was glad they were all gone now. I could breathe now, in lieu of suffocating.

Emo was more determined and more resolute with Mother. "Sylvie, I know we don't know each other well. But you promised you would tell me what is going on."

Mother set her drink down on a coaster, and Marcella looked at me with a sisterly smugness. Sylvie took a cleansing breath, avoiding eye contact with all of us as Kevin moved to sit at my mother's feet.

Emo shook her head. "I don't understand. Kevin doesn't like strangers." She lifted her lovely eyes at my mother.

"I am not a stranger," Mother said. "I purchased Kevin for Leo…" She cleared her throat. "I surprised Leonard with Kevin seven years ago."

Emo nodded. "He told me he bought him in Connecticut."

"The breeder was in Connecticut. The sire was a four-time champion. We had planned—"

Emo interrupted harshly, "You had planned what? To lie to everyone who loved you both?"

Mother appeared drenched in disgrace, unable even to lift her chin off her broken heart. She shook her bowed head and whimpered, "You can't understand."

Emo retaliated, "Help us understand! My dad is dead! Your children's father is in prison for killing him, and now…" Emo's voice cracked and strained out, "And now, we are being hidden in a luxurious, *secret* penthouse because our lives are in danger! Explain it! Explain this place! Explain this!"

Emo snatched the folded note off the coffee table and tossed it at my mother.

Mother barely glanced at it and then said, "It got ugly."

Emo huffed and folded her arms across her chest and then yelled at Kevin, "Get over here and sit, you worthless mass of fur! Have some freaking loyalty!" Kevin begrudgingly moved to Emo's side, turning back at my mother with a look of true longing. A tear came tumbling out of Emo's eye, and she swatted at it with irritation.

My mother continued. "Leonard and I met when you girls were young. Emo, you were sixteen and attending dance school in London that year." Emo nodded. "Your grandmother had just passed away. Leonard had season tickets to the philharmonic. I had noticed him the year before, always doting on his mother. One night, after the concert, I stopped him on the street and asked him how she was doing. I was just… I-I inquired as to why his mother wasn't with him. He explained that she had passed away." Mother dabbed at her eyes with a handkerchief.

"Tom and you girls were away on a father-daughter trip to Florida," she continued, and I bit back tears, unwilling to break down, recalling the spontaneous beach trip and its long-lost, happy memories. "I was lonely. Leonard was lonely. We went to a coffee shop and just talked for hours. We agreed to meet the next day for lunch, and the next day we met again." Mother picked her glass up and polished off her Cosmo. "And then, he kissed me."

"We were in love." She sniffled. "And then Tom and the girls came home, and I told him."

"Told him what?" I demanded.

"I told him I was in love with someone else. That I wanted to end our marriage and have shared custody of you girls. I told him he could have the house and half of my inheritance. One hundred forty-seven million dollars."

"Half of 147 million dollars?" Emo gasped.

Marcella snorted and my mother said, "No, that's half of what I had received. And I told him he could have that and the businesses. I approached him with the facts, like a business proposal, because that is Tom's language."

My heart physically hurt. My poor dad. I felt a twinge of anger at my mother's depiction of him. He was all business, but he was also funny, loving, and warm. I finally asked, "What did Dad say?"

Mother inhaled, her breathing a jagged mix of sobs and whimpers, and finally said, "He said *no*." Which did sound exactly like something my dad would say. But then she continued. "Tom said he didn't want to do that to our girls and that I could do as I please, as long as he didn't have to know about it." Her voice cracked and strained. "He said, all that mattered is that I was happy and loved. He set up an allowance for me to maintain this place. And we went about our lives."

Emo interjected, "Then why is my dad dead?"

I followed her fury with, "And why is Dad in prison, Mother?"

Mother groaned and continued, "Two years ago, Tom asked me to end things with Leonard. One night, after we had attended an event at the club, we came home and were having a nightcap in the formal living room, and Tom…" She sobbed. "Tom presented me with a small box." She pulled a gold chain out from beneath her blouse with a small anniversary band hanging from it. She played with the diamond-encrusted band and spoke, "He asked me if I would consider helping him make our marriage what I needed, what we both needed. He had proposed it before when Bo was born and again after Davy. But this time, he said it would be different. And even the way he proposed it convinced me. He was gentle and apologetic. He said…" She sobbed for a few moments. "Tom said we were too old, and we had too much ahead of us. He wanted to travel with Bo and Davy *as a family*.

"So, you ended it with my dad?" Emo asked.

Mother shook her head. "It wasn't that simple. Leonard and I were already having problems. We were fighting every time we got together."

"Why?" Marcella asked.

"Leonard… Well… I believed he was involved with someone at work. My suspicions were driving me crazy. I couldn't imagine…" She heaved. "I couldn't imagine my life without Leonard. But he was growing more distant and making excuses not to spend time with me."

Emo snorted her response. "Oh, so he wanted some dignity instead of sneaking up a service elevator to meet with a married woman? How unreasonable!"

"Emo," my mother retorted, more harshly than I was accustomed to. "Your father fully participated in our relationship. It was our decision. I didn't keep him locked in here. And he was more than willing to buy two apartments in this building when you went to college so that you could live near him when you graduated if you wanted to."

Emo softened, leaning back in her chair. "I just am *mystified* how this went on for so long. And what about…?" She stopped and then stammered to make up for what she didn't say, "I mean… I, um…"

"Tess," my mother said flatly.

"Yeah." Emo nodded. "My dad and Tess Lambert were engaged. They had announced their engagement two weeks before…" Emo trailed off, and I pounced.

"Who is Tess Lambert?" I asked, although the name seemed familiar.

"Leonard's on-again, off-again girlfriend," Mother said.

"Oh, my God! Mother!" I choked, "What is even wrong with you people?"

Mother shot me a *mom look*, and I backed down.

"Leonard was only forty-four when our affair started. He was already involved with Tess, and she was a reporter at *The Post*, so they worked together."

"Did she know?" Marcella chimed in. "Did Tess know about you two?"

"Not from lack of trying," Mother answered. "She'd follow him, and once, she saw us come into the building together—we almost always came in separately. It doesn't matter," Mother declared. "This place was the apartment my parents arranged for me when I first signed with the orchestra here. I never lived here because, well, my parents both passed the summer we purchased it, and then I met Tom."

"The key and the address," I said without intention or direction. "Why would Dad send me a message about this place? What would that have to do with Leonard's murder?"

But before my mother could answer, Emo announced, "I need you all to leave."

"Why?" Marcella asked.

"I can't do this tonight," she semi-whimpered. "I need to take Kevin out, and I can't listen to any more of this right now."

If I hadn't just screamed my head off, I would have done it again. I didn't want any more breaks in this conversation, and I was done with stories of betrayal and complacency, in lieu of real answers.

Dessert

In the kitchen, Mother busied herself. Marcella and I stood watching her, both processing the revelations but still not up to speed on why everything was such a disaster. And whether everyone else had had enough or not, I wasn't about to toddle off to bed until I understood how an affair my dad knew about landed him in prison for the rest of his natural life.

"Mother!" I demanded. "I don't care what Emo wants. I want the rest of the story!"

Mother turned from the sink and leaned against the counter. "I don't know how to even begin. It was so awful…. It's still so awful." She slipped her hands into the pocket of her skirt; her tidy hair was falling out of the hairpin and framing her delicate features. Suddenly, I felt sorry for her. After all these months of confusion and chaos, I felt nothing but sadness for the suffering my mother had gone through. My dad, locked up in prison, but also the loss of Leonard… such a violent end.

"Mom," I said empathetically. "This whole time, you have been mourning Pruitt on top of Dad's conviction, taking care of the businesses, the house, and the boys? Were you not ever going to say anything?"

Mother shook her head. "No. That was what your father and I agreed to."

My eyes grew wide. "What do you mean?" I nearly howled.

Mother moved to the breakfast nook—a round table and bench in the corner of the kitchen. The space was cozy, with plush, black velvet cushions and braided, gold cording. She slid onto the bench, hitting a switch on the wall and illuminating the small, intricately detailed chandelier over the table. Marcella followed her, carrying a plate full of baby carrots. I hobbled to them and sat next to Marcella.

"Like I said, I agreed to try and make things better for Tom and me. It wasn't hard—Leonard and I were struggling. And Tom and I do love each other. I do…" She faltered. "I do love Tom. I always have. And things with Leonard and I were getting more and more complicated. He wanted me to leave Tom. And…" She steadied herself. "When Davy was born, Leonard wanted to build a life together with me. *No babies.*"

Marcella crunched on a carrot, and I turned to see if she had any idea what was going on. Mother continued. "That wasn't ever going to happen. I wouldn't have done that to Tom or Davy. And Bo!" she piped. "Leonard wanted to create this fairy tale where I wasn't over sixty years old and a custodial grandparent."

Marcella stopped chewing. "That's an elaborate swing!"

Mother nodded. "Yes. Honestly, it was preposterous. It didn't make any sense. When Bo was born, things had gotten hard for Leonard and me. He was jealous of Tom and me, and he was very unhappy about a newborn being added to the mix of our romance. But then things settled down." She shook her head. "Then Davy came along. By then,

Leonard and I had been together eleven years. He had this need, this desire for us to create something different. When I wouldn't leave Tom, he ended our affair. We were separated for ten months, and he and Tess started dating again. But I wanted him back. So, when Davy was one, I got Leonard a dog."

I snorted. "Perfect."

"Think what you want, Clara," Mother huffed. "It did work. Leonard was lonely. He and Tess never really connected. And I don't say that because I was jealous. He was never happy with her, and he always wanted more with me. Kevin placated him, and in a lot of ways, that dog drew Leonard and me closer together."

"How's that?" I asked.

"It was this illusion of family, I guess. That dog was something common we cared for and worked for—together." Mother twisted her watch on her tiny wrist. "For a while, Kevin was something that we could progress in. You can only have hot sex and secret rendezvous for so long before... Well, there was always this space where Leonard and I didn't progress."

I laughed. "Yeah, I guess—"

She cut me off. "Don't, Clara. Please." She dropped her head. "I can't possibly feel more horrified than I already do. Tom always said, *A little powder, a little paint, makes a girl look what she ain't!*" She sniffled and a giggle escaped her. "After Kevin's last title win, Leonard decided he was done with the dog show circuit. So, three years ago, he began pressuring me to leave, to assign custody of Bo and Davy to Tom, and then Leonard and I would move away together and start fresh. He was ready to tell Emo everything." Mother drummed her fingers on the table. "Every time we met, we fought. And Tom knew how much I was suffering."

IN LIEU OF EATING

"You and Dad talked about this?" I asked incredulously.

"No, no, not like that. Tom just knows me." She drummed her fingers again and then folded her hands. "So, as I said, Tom suggested we start fresh two years ago. But he had secrets too."

"Dad?" Marcella chimed in.

"Yes. Well, not an affair. But I suspected something when Honey's bid for the 57th location went through so quickly. Leonard was the first to point it out. That location was highly coveted. And there was no bidding war. Leonard started following Tom. He told me he thought Tom might be laundering money for Alito." Mother hugged herself, rocking a little as tears rolled down her cheeks. "But I decided that for Bo's and Davy's sake, I would stand by my commitment and make things better for Tom and me."

"And?" I demanded.

"And," she continued, "Leonard and Tess started being seen around town again, holding hands. Leonard would text me as he moved things out of the penthouse. We basically avoided each other. We were cordial in public and toxic in private. But when your father told me to come to the restaurant for a surprise on my birthday, I was excited to start a new chapter with Tom."

"But the party wasn't for you," I whispered.

"No. He forgot. And I left that evening and…I went to Leonard. That was Thursday. On Friday morning, Tom and I fought again, and I told him I was leaving him and starting a new life with Leonard. I called Leonard, and he said…" She moaned. "He said, he was no longer in love with me. That he felt sorry for me the night before because it was my birthday. I was humiliated. And so, I threatened to take Kevin."

"*You threatened to take the man's dog?*" I yelped.

Mother nodded. "But it gets worse. Tom and I never discussed Alito, but I knew that Alito had some shady connections because, like

I said, Leonard had been following them. I saw Leonard at the grand opening of the restaurant. We were cordial, put on the appropriate appearances. But I followed Leonard to the parking garage when he left, and I threatened him again." Now Mother was blubbering. "I told him I would take Kevin and that I held the dog's papers as his rightful owner if Leonard left me. He said he hated me. And that I was ridiculous. Leonard said if I tried to take Kevin, he would expose me and Tom. He said he had proof that Tom was laundering money for Alito. I ran from him, and when I went back upstairs, and I bumped into Alito Senior in the corridor, I just..." She sobbed. "I just asked him to get Kevin. I told him I was the rightful owner."

"You wanted a dog?" Marcella chimed in with horrific timing.

"No, not at all. It was just nonsense. I just felt humiliated and foolish. I guess I thought that if I had Kevin, and Leonard and I could just talk, none of this would have to be so... *awful*." She blew her nose. "Leonard was not supposed to be hurt. But Alito sent Low to get Kevin from Leonard." She dropped her head and wailed out in remorse, "Low beat Leonard nearly to death." She choked and heaved. "Tom called me and said he was coming to get me. It was an emergency. We took a cab to the warehouse—our warehouse in the West Village. Alito and Low were there. Kevin was tied to a pole by his lead. Leonard was tied to a chair—he was unrecognizable. We couldn't even tell if he was breathing." She sobbed and then said, "Alito said that when Low attempted to take Kevin, Leonard caught him, and they fought." Mother dropped her face in her hands, lamenting the tragedy. Finally, she sat up straight, sniffed, and began speaking again matter-of-factly. "Alito said that it went too far. Low had been sloppy. So, they brought Leonard to our warehouse and called us to come." She wiped her nose as Marcella crunched and I bit back horror.

She drummed her fingers yet again and said, "Low pulled out a gun, walked over to Leonard, and shot him...." She shuddered. "Low

Alito shot Leonard in front of us, in the head." She groaned now, sobbing at the memory. "He... he wiped down the gun and then tossed it at Tom. Tom just stood there holding it, shaking. Alito Sr. said, 'Tom, this is no longer my problem.' Tom had the gun with his fingerprints on it. Alito and Low left, and we were alone in the warehouse with my lover's dead body."

"This has to be the dumbest scenario imaginable, Mother!" I squawked.

"Eh-hm," Marcella interjected. "It's the second-dumbest scenario. Remember, you thought Emo and I were twins separated at birth a little while ago."

"What?" my mother gasped.

"It was a theory I was working on," I spat.

"Clara," my mother sniffled. "Darling, you really need to get out and meet some people your own age."

"Oh, my god! Is there a hidden camera somewhere? Is someone recording this?" I yelled into the air. "You people are insane! *Insane!* The whole lot of you are lunatics, and the only one of us with an ounce of integrity or any kind of moral compass is in jail for killing a man none of you killed! *Over a dog?*"

"And probably some money laundering," Marcella chirped.

"Marcella..." I turned to face her. "Shut up. Do not say another single word, or there are not enough designer red-bottom shoes on the planet that will stop me from killing you with my bare hands."

Marcella nodded and continued munching on carrots. I glared at her, contempt, and raw, unbridled mystification at how she could snack on carrot sticks as our mother confessed to hiring a hit on her lover's Irish Setter, *Kevin.*

I huffed, then ripped the cuff off my neck and tossed it.

My mother breathed, "Honey, don't you think...?"

I stretched my neck, reveling in the tenderness, and stopped her. "Don't I think what? That I should sit helplessly while my father rots in prison *because of you?*"

"Clara." My mother's voice was harsher now. "I made a horrible mistake. I can't fix that. But your father and I didn't know what to do. We were at the warehouse, no car, and I begged Tom to call the police so that we could end this nightmare."

"*Then why didn't you?*" I pressed.

"Tom said that he and Alito had never had any illegal dealings. They just played tennis. But then, Tom mentioned to Alito that you, Clara, had bid on 57th Street. Within hours, you won the bid, and your father now owed Alito. At first, he didn't ask for anything, but then Alito showed up at the downtown office with an enormous amount of cash that needed…processing. The only way to do that was for Tom to run the money through our businesses." She sighed. "Tom said that if we called the police, you could lose the restaurant and your reputation would be ruined. Both of us could end up in prison, or Alito would kill him, possibly me…you girls…the boys."

Marcella crunched on a carrot.

Mother began again. "Tom sent me to JFK by cab from the warehouse. I rented a car. By then, it was nearly eleven o'clock at night. And we knew Leonard would be missed at work Monday morning, if Tess wasn't already wondering about him. Leonard wouldn't have been seen since the grand opening of the restaurant. Your father put Leonard in the trunk and told me to go to the penthouse in a cab with Kevin. I was to log into Leonard's desktop, which is still in the penthouse office, and submit a negative review of your restaurant. Then, I was to email his boss, pretending to be Leonard, and tell him Leonard had food poisoning from eating at Honey's."

"*You wrote that review?*" I shrieked.

"Yes. I know. It didn't even sound like Leonard. I copied and pasted most of it from another review I found online."

"Yeah, I mean, what's a little plagiarism at this point, right?" I snarked.

My mother narrowed her eyes at me, and again, I backed off. "Your father disposed of Leonard's body, returned the car, and we waited. If Leonard wasn't found, we would just… I don't know what. Really, Emo would have wanted answers, so the issue wasn't just going to fade away. Oh, and Tess… She would have looked for Leonard, *I promise.*" Her voice had become a whimper. "But being that Tom had no real experience with disposing of bodies…"

"Leonard was found Thursday morning, after the article ran," I said flatly.

"Yes," Mother agreed. "Tom told me that he would confess. No one would ever have to know about the affair. I would raise the boys, and he would accept the consequences of our actions."

"This is outer limits, Mother!" I was clamoring to even understand how these two people who I call Mom and Dad had been running on fumes for so long to keep up appearances.

My mother tapped a single finger on the table. "Stop!" she spat. "It is worse than I could have ever even imagined. I don't need to be scolded. What would you have us do? Orphan two innocent boys? Have them be uprooted because their gram and poppy were criminals? I followed your father's instructions to the letter. I assume he left the message for you or for whoever about the penthouse in case things began to spiral further out of control! Which they obviously have!"

"*Because of me!*" I fumed. "Because I wouldn't let Dad stay in prison for something he is incapable of doing?"

"What's going on?" Emo stood in the doorway in purple satin paisley pajamas, a matching scarf tied around her head.

DESSERT

Mother dropped her head. And Marcella poured more wine into her glass and eyed everyone in the room like a spectator at a sporting event. If we weren't in protective custody, she'd be the belle of the ball on the New York gossip scene.

I looked at Emo and back at my mother. "*Tell her!*"

Emo folded her arms, and Kevin sauntered in and lay at her feet. "Tell me what?"

"Maybe you should sit down." My mother scooted further into the bench.

"What's going on?"

My mother patted the bench, and Emo softened and moved across the kitchen to join her. Kevin begrudgingly followed.

"Tom didn't kill Leonard. And no one was hired to kill your father. Tom would have never caused anyone this much suffering. He's not capable." Mother's voice was calm now. Emo's shoulders slumped.

Mother proceeded to tell Emo of the end of the affair and her tragic idea to ask Alito to take Kevin. Marcella continued to eat carrots. She ate them until they were gone like potato chips. Except they weren't chips. They were carrots.

When my mother was finished, Emo's breath was jagged and shallow, like she might hyperventilate. After several moments, my mother touched Emo's folded hands. "Emo? Are you okay?"

"No," she whispered. "Yeah. And no. I hate that he suffered. I love that he fought." Emo closed her eyes. Pulling her hands from my mother, she folded her arms.

"It's hard for me." Emo exhaled. "My dad, I knew he had secrets. This is the tragic part. Learning about this man who I know better now that he's gone."

My mother clutched her chest and whispered in French, "*Est-ce qu'il me détest?*"

IN LIEU OF EATING

Does he hate me...?

A tear escaped Emo's eye and rolled down her cheek, landing on her pajamas. She closed her eyes and inhaled deeply, then answered in flawless French, "*Il n'est pas capable de haine. Il est amour et lumière.*"

He is not capable of hate. He is love and light. And Emo lay her head on my mother's shoulder. She whimpered a bit and then lifted her head. "Thank you for telling me. May I ask a question?"

My mother nodded and whispered, "Yes."

Emo sniffled out, "When this is cleared up, is it your intention to take Kevin from me?"

"*No! No!* No, I am so sorry, Emo. No, of course not. Kevin is yours. That was a quarrel between Leonard and me. I never wanted any of this. I am so sorry. You shouldn't have to suffer any more for my foolishness."

Emo let out a faint chuckle. "Thank you. I wouldn't want to have to cut you to ribbons, but I would if you tried to take my dog."

We would have laughed, but the intimate confessional of the breakfast nook was disturbed by a loud bang at the door. We slipped out of the nook, and Mother, Marcella, and Emo left Kevin and me to see who was at the door. I assumed it was Axel, finally back from the gym, or the officer coming to escort Emo and Kevin outside. But the sounds from the foyer were not friendly. Kevin raised his ears quizzically, then barked once and retreated under the table.

"What are you so afraid of, you big baby?" I asked just as my mother, Marcella, and Emo entered the kitchen at gunpoint, with Lorenzo Alito Senior standing behind the speechless trio. "I imagine he's pretty afraid of me," Alito spat, lowering the gun and pointing it directly at me. "As you should be, *Honey*. Where is my son?"

I wasn't afraid of guns or Alito. I just wanted my life back. "He's in the morgue," I said flatly, then boldly limped to the fridge, ignoring the gun. "He came after me. So, we killed him."

DESSERT

Marcella looked at me as if her eyes were about to pop right out as Alito pulled the hammer back on the gun he still had aimed at my head.

"I really don't care if you kill me," I announced, removing a bottle of cranberry juice from the top shelf of the fridge, then shutting the fridge door and calmly whirling to face him. "Kill all of us. There are only so many bodies you can hide. At least my dad would be exonerated."

"You are a real piece of work, kid." He snorted. "How about I kill you last, and you sit there and watch me pluck off your family one by one?"

I huffed, which sounded much braver than I was feeling. "Fine but start with Marcella." I grabbed a glass from a low shelf and set it on the counter. "Maybe, eventually, you'll get to someone I actually give a shit about." I poured a glass full of cranberry juice and took a sip, never taking my eyes off him.

"Well…," he chuckled. "I took care of that cop and your driver-boyfriend." I steadied myself, horrified that Axel was in fact injured, but I held my stare. Alito looked around the kitchen and whistled. Kevin looked up, and Alito swung the gun down toward the dog and fired. Mother and Emo screamed. The rocket blast of the gun continued to explode in echoes of sharp pain in my ears. Disoriented, I watched as Kevin collapsed, blood pouring from his neck.

"Shut up!" Alito yelled just as Davy came wandering into the kitchen. "Hello, little man!" Alito hissed and pulled the hammer back on the gun as adrenaline coursed through my veins.

Clunk!

There was a crash, and Alito fell face down on the kitchen floor with a heavy thump. The gun flew from his hands and slid under the breakfast table. His thick, gray hair was quickly consumed by a mass of blood, and we all stood speechless as Bo, who had smacked Alito over the head with a marble cherub, stood in his boxer shorts and tube socks over our attacker, his body shaking.

"You guys okay?" he panted. Alito started to stir. He got his hands and feet under him, lifting up on all fours, trying to stand. Before anyone could react, Marcella reached under the table, picked up the gun, and shot Alito in the chest. Alito's white shirt turned scarlet, and he dropped with a shuddering gasp back onto the floor.

Mother leaped into action and hit the alarm on the wall. The entire place lit up with flashing lights and wailing noises. Emo rushed to Kevin's side, screaming, "*No!* Please, *no!*"

"Marcella, call 911," Mother told Marcella in a rush. "They'll already be on their way but tell them what happened so they can be ready." She turned to me. "Take Davy—go into Emo's room. It has a television and a fridge. Just take care of Davy! *Go!*"

Davy was bleary-eyed, white with shock, and I grabbed his hand and led him away from the blood and tragedy. "Wait!" I turned to my mother. "*Axel!*"

Marcella pulled the phone away from her ear and said, "I will find him. *I promise.* Go, please, get my baby out of here." Our eyes locked, and she said, "I need you to take care of Davy."

"Okay. Yeah, okay," I muttered. The chaos still vibrating in my bones, I guided Davy down the hall to Emo's room.

We stayed there, Davy and I, watching *The Parent Trap* in silence, waiting for everything to be okay again. Occasionally, I would open the door and peer down the hall. I saw paramedics and police and listened to a cacophony of rushed footfalls mixed with urgent, efficient voices, then I texted Marcella, asking for an update.

Marcella texted back: *I'll be there when I can.*

Finally, Davy fell asleep, and I limped down the hallway, desperate to know if Axel was okay and to see if there was any news on Kevin.

DESSERT

Emo sat on the chaise lounge, sobbing, Marcella holding her as Emo grieved and begged, "Please, I just need to go and check on him."

Mother was in the kitchen with Detective Cassum. Blood had pooled and streaked across the floor, not yet dry. "Mother, where is Axel?" I pleaded.

Cassum stepped toward me. "Axel's okay. He was shot in his left shoulder. He's been taken to the hospital and is in stable condition."

"The officer from the elevator?" I asked.

"He was wearing a vest." Cassum patted his chest. "He's okay."

I looked at my mother. "Bo?"

She grinned. "Asleep."

Emo and Marcella ran into the kitchen with Emo joyfully weeping. "Kevin!" she squealed. "He's okay! They are taking him to surgery, but *he's okay!*"

Mother dropped her head and wept.

Detective Cassum pulled his phone out of his pocket and declared, "Well, that's enough for tonight. Why don't we let forensics get in here to finish up, and you folks get some rest? I'll be back in the morning, and we can continue with statements."

My mother nodded, and Emo said, "Will you take me to the animal hospital on 44th? I just need to be there when Kevin is out of surgery."

"Yeah, sure," Cassum agreed.

"Should I go to the hospital and check on Axel?" I asked no one in particular.

Marcella interjected, "I have talked to him and to his cousin, who is flying in tonight to help."

"Oh," I said. "So…what? We just go to bed now? Is Alito dead? Is Marcella in trouble? Is my dad going to get out of prison?"

Detective Cassum chuckled. "Yeah, that's exactly right. You just go to bed now. Alito is dead, but Marcella isn't in trouble, although she has probably met her quota of defense killings. We can talk about what happens next tomorrow." He turned to my mother and did that bow thing. "You'll probably want to invite your attorney."

Mother nodded and escorted Cassum to the door. Marcella and I moved to Emo's room where Davy slept peacefully.

"Now what?" I wondered, just standing there in half a daze.

"I guess we go to bed?" She snorted. She looked at Davy, all curled up in a tiny ball in the middle of the enormous mattress, engulfed by huge blankets. "I doubt Emo will be back." She sighed. "I think I will curl up with my guy."

I watched Marcella as she crept into the bed, fully clothed in her high school jeans and Kermit shirt. She kicked off her sneakers and nuzzled her nose into Davy's neck. Davy turned his body, rolling into Marcella's embrace. He sighed and mumbled, "Hey Aunt Markie. Did you have another bad dream?"

"Not this time, buddy. I just needed to be close to you."

I stood in amazement as she kissed his cheeks and smelled his head. Davy whispered, "Sing me our song." And Marcella began to croon the old Jennings and Nelson song, *"Mammas, don't let your babies grow up to be cowboys..."*

And I left. I didn't want to be alone, but more than that, I didn't want to impose any more of my opinions or nonsensical critiques on my family. I wandered into the den where my mother stood at the window, her skirt rumpled, her tussled hair illuminated by city lights. I watched her sip brandy for a while, then cleared my throat to alert her of my presence.

She turned, her face streaked with tears, and looked at me adoringly. "*Clara,*" she sighed. "Oh, Clara, what a tangled mess I've weaved." She hiccup-sobbed.

DESSERT

I limped toward her. "Mom...I am so sorry that you have suffered so much loss in the last months. I wish..." I didn't have an appropriate wish at the moment.

She smiled softly and turned back to face the city. "It has been lonely. Secrets always are."

"What's going to happen?"

She didn't turn to face me, just looked out at the city. "I'm sure there will be consequences, but Lance and Rose believe that Tom will be somewhat exonerated. There was still illegal activity on both our parts."

I stepped closer to her and lay my head on her shoulder. We stared at the city as the sun began to peep over the horizon in blazes of pink and orange. My mother wrapped her arm around me. "For now, let's just rest in the promise of a new day. No more secrets. No more violence," she purred.

And we watched the sun rise, in lieu of hiding in the dark.

Mignardise

Eleven Months Later...

Many years back, I had filed a noise complaint against a band next door to my first restaurant location. The officer who took the call had sat the lead singer and me down to talk out my grievances.

"It's just too loud," I complained. But he explained, the entire building was double-insulated, and I wasn't hearing loud music. I was *feeling* the bass, and my ears confused the sensation for sound. To prove his point, he went next door, turned the bass up, and came back to my restaurant.

"I told you!" I griped to the officer. "It's too loud!"

And the musician said, "Record it with your phone."

I did as he asked and hit the record button, but when we played it back, there was no pounding music. The band leader folded his arms and huffed, "You have your senses mixed up, chef! Look up from your prep table. You're missing the good parts."

In the months after the attack, and after learning the truth about Leonard Pruitt's death, I often thought of that band leader. There was no grand revelation, and I will probably never be coined a hero. But in my lack of perception, my senses became organized. I got it; pain and suffering often negate taste, smell, touch, and hearing. I did let those senses be drowned in the wake of loss. I don't chastise myself for that, nor do I wish that none of it ever happened. Those happenings awakened the appropriate senses.

Prior to that, I had drowned my senses out with my weak attempts at a brash facade, hiding in the kitchen, where I created dishes designed to distract and impress nobody, really, but myself. The distraction: that everyone was beneath me. The impression: I had what they wanted. It seems silly now. I suppose I imposed my ability to master spice on my sister, squelching her show of real self, her authenticity. I confess, I believe it was more out of jealousy than contempt. It isn't that I condone abandoning your sons or having no godly idea who their fathers are.

However, those faults—if one chooses to see them that way—were not mine to carry. And maybe that is what I learned. Love is easy; it is the natural consequence of being together as a family. All the rest of it is an illusion we create that isolates us and turns us into the worst kind of contributor—a self-righteous one. Sounds more like a wasp than a honeybee.

Dad will serve the next five-to-seven years in a minimum-security prison. Marcella, the boys, and I go see him every other Sunday. My mother was charged with a variety of misdemeanors, but Lance Vega was able to exonerate her of one felony count based on lack of intent. Most of the charges were waived in exchange for her testimony, which closed the books on the Alitos' criminal activities. Well, that, and the deaths of Junior and Senior.

Marcella moved home to help Mother with the boys. I returned to my flat, got a psychiatrist and a personal trainer, joined a recovery group, and begged for another chance at *The Fork*. My pleas were denied. So, I decided to start my own online food magazine. *Honey's Taste and See* is on its third issue. I have 790 subscribers and nine thousand Instagram followers. Marcella works part-time for me, handling all my graphics, marketing, photos, and editing.

Mother goes to see my dad on the Sundays that Marcella and I stay home with the boys. I am not sure what will happen when Dad gets home. But at least we have a chance of something honest when he does.

Emo and Kevin are around quite often. Kevin walks a little crooked but otherwise recovered nicely. Emo sold her gallery and decided to go back to school, pursuing a graduate degree at NYU in religious studies. Recently, she joined us for dinner, and my mother asked her about the decision. Emo explained that spirituality intrigues her now more than ever. She wanted to take some time to really understand how we get so caught up in our humanity, how we neglect the spiritual parts and miss out on the good stuff for the pomp and circumstance.

I'd have to agree. And because of that fact, and the fact that I don't have the patience for school, I often enjoy thought-provoking conversations with Emo about organized religion, politics, and culture. It was during one of our coffee-house chats, after a day at the museum, that I remembered her recurring compliment, "I enjoy your mind."

That is the piece that was missing. I judged actions on my personal scale of scorn, and I forgot to use my mind to direct my heart.

One day, the conversation led to the power of the arts on political discourse, and Emo mentioned Marcella's show, *One Cobalt Blue Shot of Tequila*. I want to get it, but I just don't, though I have watched it so many times, my eyes might start bleeding. I confessed this to Emo.

MIGNARDISE

"I mean, I get the exposed body and spirit thing. But why that? Why the cowboy boot? The Pepsi cans?"

Emo shook her lovely head. "I'm not going to answer that for you. Don't grapple with it. Art means different things to different people. That's what makes it art. Now, if you want to discuss what I experienced, we can talk about that. But I am not going to answer your questions with my experiences."

Emo Pruitt.

Stone. Cold. Goddess.

She has no equal. Emo's balanced and sane. And she is strong and driven. But I don't need to catch up to her. Emotional growth is not a foot race.

Emo continued, "I saw Marcella's show as a cry for attention, but not in a negative or greedy way. I respect the nudity because, for one thing, that girl is tight." We both laughed. "But more than that, it was the last of her. It was as far as she could take what she was saying and make the point."

"The point being?"

She shook her head again. "Well, *for me*, the point was that we are all the same. A spirit in a body. The body does the damage or is a victim of the damage. The spirit remains."

I smiled. "I get what you're saying, that is what you got from it. I understand."

"So," she continued, "even if you didn't like it, what do you take away from it?"

I considered this for a few moments. "Well, I take away that Marcella is brave. Does it have to be more than that?"

"Not if that applies to you."

I remembered what Emo had said that day in the park: "*I know Marcella in the ways that matter to me.*" And I suddenly wanted a movie poster of my sister's show hung neatly in my flat. Not because I liked the show but because it was my sister's art. It was a testament to what I took away from her show, a newfound love and understanding of my family in the ways that matter for me.

Axel returned to Argentina with his cousin almost immediately after being released from the hospital. We text constantly, and I have much regret, but I am not sure how to go about making things right. Or what right might look like.

"Go see him!" Marcella squawked.

"Just show up in Argentina, unannounced and profess…what?" I shook my head, unsure.

"That you want some coochie-coo!" She poked at me.

"You're an idiot."

"That might be true. But you have no sense of romance or adventure."

I sat down on the sofa of my flat while Marcella sank into my fancy green chair.

"This chair is so uncomfortable. Why don't you replace it?"

"I love that chair. It's beautiful."

Marcella huffed, "You can have both, you know. Looks and comfort." She winked at me, shoving an outrageously huge piece of cake in her mouth.

"Hey!" I yelped. "Did you already take pictures of that?"

"Yes," she mumbled. "This is really good. You could get rich off this stuff."

"I already am rich, stupid."

"Maybe that's your problem."

"How's that, Miss I Have Twenty-Four Different Gucci Ace Bandages?"

"Well, what are you doing all this for if not for money? Or to impress Dad or the masses? Or whatever? What do you want?"

I didn't know. Something still didn't fit. The pieces were falling into place, but there was something missing.

"Damn." Marcella stood and took her plate to the sink, texting with her free hand.

"What?"

"BO11." She huffed. "I'm on it."

Marcella grabbed her bag and slipped on her shoes. "I'll deal with this, and I'll get these photos edited and put them in the drop box for you. Are you posting on Instagram tomorrow or me?"

I didn't answer her, staring at my phone, my eyes blurred at the last text Axel sent: *How are Bo and Davy?*

"Honey?" Marcella quizzed me.

"Huh?" I shook myself back into cognition.

"Are you posting on Instagram, or am I?"

"Oh." I thought for a minute. *What am I doing this for?* "Yeah…you know what?"

"What?"

"Marcella, I need you to take over for me for a few days."

"Oh, my god," she said flatly. "Are you going to Argentina?"

I inhaled, not ready to say what I was thinking out loud but in too deep to just disappear.

"Yeah. But it isn't what you think."

"Probably not. I have a pretty raunchy imagination," she chirped. "What are you now, thirty-three? I think it's time for you to get some action."

"Marcella, I hate to break it to you, but I have had lovers."

Marcella cackled. "Oh, really? Oh! No, you can't count Ronnie Mason getting under your bra on that field trip in junior high. That's not a lover, that's copping a feel."

"For your information, while studying pastry in Rome, I had a steamy affair with one of my instructors."

"Liar."

"Sorry, sis. I did not break my nose skiing in France. I broke my nose in a disastrous attempt at page nineteen of the Kama Sutra."

"Shut up." Marcella's eyes bugged out. "*The Kama Sutra?*"

"I know stuff." I smirked. "For instance, I know that if you don't go find your son, Mother is going to freak out."

"Oh, he's fine. He just got caught cheating again. I want to hear more about this Italian lover. What did he look like?"

"I never said *he* was *Italian*," I retorted, lying through my teeth. "Get out." I then grabbed my sister by her slim upper arms and kissed her abruptly on both cheeks. "Take care of Mom and tell Dad I will come see him in two weeks."

"Fine." Marcella pulled the door open and then turned back to me, true concern on her beautiful face. "Clara, do you…? Um, what if Axel…? You know?"

"What?"

"What if he's met someone?"

I considered this for a second and then said, "I don't care. I'm still going. Not to profess my love or ask him to return with me. He's already said, he doesn't feel that way about me." I sighed, a twinge of humiliation nipping at me. "I have known Axel since I was twenty-two. He's my friend, and I want to see him. I want to see him in his element. I want to thank him for being such a good friend and apologize for not noticing him sooner."

Marcella nodded. "Okay but promise me you'll let me know you're okay."

"I promise." I gave her a gentle push out the common door of my flat.

"I love you," she piped, and as I closed the door, she yelped, "I want details! You owe me! I saved your life, you know!"

Yeah, you did, I thought as I began to throw a few things in my suitcase and confirmed a flight to Buenos Aires for 6 p.m. this evening on the app on my phone.

I called a car service and made hotel arrangements on the way to the airport. No matter what would happen with Axel, I would use this time to my benefit. I booked the prettiest room I could find, with a stunning view and room service. Sixteen hours later, I was in another car headed to the hotel. My heart had not stopped pounding, and I considered a snort of something from the mini fridge. But in lieu of using alcohol to cope, I primped.

It was one o'clock, and I was feeling travel-weary but eager to lay eyes on Axel, and possibly my hands and mouth too. But one thing at a time. I took a luxurious shower, breathing in the rose-scented body wash and plotting. It wasn't going to be an ambush, but I felt the pangs of worst-case scenarios marching through my brain, along with the hopeful rush of a romantic interlude. Which made me scroll through all the same mental questions again.

I picked a yellow sundress with tiny, embroidered green leaves on the bodice and a flowing, loosely knit shawl to cover my somewhat more toned but still kind of thick arms. I had made a habit of regularly tending to my eyebrows, and I wondered if Axel had ever seen me so wide-eyed. I began to style my curls on top of my head and then opted to let them fly wild. Something I was certain Axel had never seen. My curls had grown longer and were in excellent condition since rekindling my relationship with Marcella, who not only had her lovely fingers in my business, but she also kept them artfully in my hair pretty much daily.

I turned and checked my butt in the reflection and noticed my hair was much longer than I had realized, tumbling to the middle of my waist. I applied a dab of blush and a few swipes of mascara, then pressed my lips together to spread a shimmer of gloss. Then I proceeded to talk to myself in the reflection.

"*Honesty. Joy. Love. It's okay.*"

And I went down to meet a cab to go see my friend, Axel Delgado.

Showing up unannounced was probably a mistake. But when the cab pulled up in front of a three-story, white stucco townhouse, there was no turning back. On the porch in the front of the house sat Axel. He was wearing running shorts and a soaking-wet white t-shirt that clung to every part of his muscular body. The glow on his face and the familiar smile jabbed at me. And I noticed, *He's just back from a run.*

Before I could make my quick escape back into the cab, I also noticed the woman in the second chair on the porch at the same unfortunate time Axel noticed me. Drenched in sweat, drinking from a sports bottle, was the most beautiful woman I think the universe ever created. She was tropical, with jet-black hair in a long ponytail; huge, almond-shaped eyes; golden skin; and full, rosy lips. The couple both stood, staring at me. I imagined I looked so silly, standing there all dolled up in a sundress and Birkenstocks on the street. Axel said something to the woman and then strolled toward me.

"What are you doing here, Clara?"

"I came to see you," I mumbled, humiliation and regret barking at me from behind.

"Why?"

"I…" I struggled. "You left so fast, and I wanted to see you." I cleared my throat. "I should have called, I guess."

Axel looked back over his shoulder at the woman on the porch and then back at me. "You look good," he remarked.

"Thank you." Then I explained, "I did all the things you suggested."

"You're running?" Axel gasped.

"God, no! I mean, I have been healing. Not drinking. You know, just getting to know me. Getting to know what I want."

"That's good." Axel shuffled his feet and folded his arms, looking between me and the Latino goddess on the porch.

"Look, Axel…" I decided it was time to let him off the hook and go about my vacation. "I didn't come here to make things weird. I came to thank you."

"For what?"

"For being my friend. For looking out for me and my family. For putting up with our crap."

He laughed, and I continued, "You stayed on with us and took care of us well beyond what an employee would have the common sense to do. Which can only be explained because…"

"I love you."

"What?"

"Which can only be explained because I love you."

I didn't speak, but only because I didn't want to have any lies or secrets. I steadied myself, eyeing the woman on the porch, feeling a little bit confused. "I don't want you to love me."

"Excuse me?" Axel nearly choked.

"Well, I mean, I think I love you too. But I haven't known who I am since, well, I don't think I have ever known. So, I came here healthier. At least, I think I am healthier, mentally and spiritually, to see if there is something between us now that… now that… I…"

"Now that you notice?" he finished my sentence impeccably.

"Yes." I nodded and then added, "But I understand if I am too late." I shot a quick glance at the woman on the porch who was taking a selfie and then typing something on her iPhone. I looked back at Axel who was still staring at me. "I know I came at a bad time."

IN LIEU OF EATING

Axel shook his head and whistled in a high pitch, and the woman looked up. He piped, "Valentina, tell Diego to hurry up and get out of the shower. I'm going for a walk on the beach with my friend, Honey." Valentina stood up and walked into the condo. "That's my cousin Diego's wife. We all run together," he explained.

"Oh!" I said with too much enthusiastic revelation. "Oh. *Sooo*..."

"So, let me get a shower, and I will take you to see some sights, and we can notice stuff. See what happens next. Okay?"

I smiled and nodded. "Okay."

He turned to go, and then turned back and said, "You might want to wait on the porch."

I stopped, slightly taken aback. "Okay...?"

He smiled and his dimple flashed. "My mom is inside. She doesn't care much for you."

I gushed, laughing, "Oh, yeah. She thinks we kidnapped you and made you come to New York."

"Well, that, and me getting shot... Dead people, floating in the Hudson..."

"Right. How about I meet you at the coffee shop on the corner?" I laughed.

Axel stopped walking, turned, and took my hand. "You know what? No. Come on in. Let's do this right. No secrets."

I nodded. "No secrets."

And so began a life I noticed, in lieu of all I would no longer miss.

The End

Enjoy this excerpt from
Jami Amerine's Next Novella

96 Minutes Between Seven and Eight

October 2009, Manhattan, NYC

Cozie Delacruz held the cordless phone to her ear. The phone's antenna had broken off in 1999, proving it wasn't really necessary. Ten years later, it still got the job done.

"That's right. Cosette, C-O-S-E-T-T-E, D-E-L-A-C-R-U-Z." She spoke into the receiver.

Cozie waited for the pharmacy to confirm her pick-up as she shoved random papers into her unreasonably, enormous floral shoulder bag. By chance, her index finger got caught in something gooey at the bottom of the bag. She boldly licked her finger, pleased by the taste of caramel and not mayonnaise or something worse. "Great." She volleyed with the woman on the other line. "Yes, thirty minutes. I'm leaving my studio now." Cozie shook her watch out from under layers of dangling bracelets. She noted the time, 6 pm, and then began to chew on her bottom lip, rehearsing all that needed to be done in the hours before her weary body could fall into her warm bed.

"Don't chew on your lip! You look like a mental person! Look at me when I talk to you!" Cozie's ex-husband's voice was tightly twisted in and out among the fingers of her nervous system. Quickly she admonished herself for allowing ghosts in her head.

IN LIEU OF EATING

When the ghost fired off its haunted scolding, Cozie was forced to count backward from ten, warding off the pain of losing *everything*.

As she shut off the lights, she surveyed her studio. It was a mess. But in a good way. Earlier that day, Cozie's brother, Rio, the youngest of her nine older brothers, had unloaded a U-Haul truck full of her latest abstract oil pastel series, "*Remnants of Hope.*"

The streetlights illuminated the studio. In less than twenty-four hours, Cozie would have everything in pristine order, which by the current state seemed impossible. But the *Cozie Delacruz Art Studio* grand opening event was to begin tomorrow night at 8, and nothing was going to stop her from making it the event of her bright future.

Shaking herself out of her dreamy daze, Cozie pulled on her favorite bulky, cable-knit sweater and locked the old-style factory door on her West Village studio lease. She checked the door twice and then scurried to the subway for errands and home on the east side of Manhattan.

The subway ride was uneventful, as far as subway rides go. There was a homeless man talking to himself. A younger couple got in a fight. The woman stormed off the ride leaving her date to slur obscenities at her back as the subway jerked ahead, leaving the poor fool dateless.

Cozie exited the subway at the next stop and kept her eyes down as she braved the October evening air toward the pharmacy. Inside she made her way to the back and alerted the pharmacist she was going to grab some things from the bodega next door and would be right back.

Cozie's stomach growled and gurgled, reminding her she had had nothing to eat since toast and coffee at 5 am. A shiver ran up her spine as hateful rattling of her past, once again barked in her mind. "*You're so disorganized! You're a waste of space! Why are we out of everything? You can't manage to buy bread and milk?!? You're pathetic!*"

Creep. That was the best word for Cozie's ex-husband. He was a creep and continued to creep in and out of her thoughts. Again, Cozie shook the haunting off and then murmured condolences to herself as she wandered about the bodega, gathering things for her refrigerator and empty cabinets. Tonight, she would feast on a well-balanced, perfectly portioned dinner for one, proving to Cozie that Jeffry Collins Alexander the Fourth, her miserable ex, was wrong about her. She threw sensible things in her basket, "I am not pathetic. I am joy. I am light. I am sensible. I eat hummus and carrots for dinner. I am going to eat yogurt for dessert." She continued her self-pep talk while mindlessly grabbing Cheese Puffs, jellybeans, pickles, a six-pack of beer, and a children's breakfast cereal that looked magical and delicious. She grabbed a few things for her elderly neighbor, taking a moment to look at some lip gloss at the makeup counter. She tried the sample and then admired herself in the mirror. Not bad for a thirty-something divorcee. She actually thought she looked a bit like a Mexican Julia Roberts, if her nose were narrower.

After checking out at the bodega and pharmacy, Cozie stepped out into the crispy evening, a light sprinkling of rain chased her to her building. She rattled a list of things that stood between Cozie and her marshmallow cereal, fluffy-soft pajamas, and a good night's sleep.

Her arms were trembling with fatigue. And her feet were screaming for the sweet release of stocking feet. She could almost hear her radiator chug and hum to life, warming her small apartment and comforting her like a welcome home hug.

The wind snarled and whipped little icy shards of frozen drizzle in Cozie's face. She hefted the bags up on her boney hip and burrowed her face in her flouncy scarves. Two more blocks, she whispered, two more blocks to *home*.

Home vibrated in her chilled bones. Her home was 980 square feet of bliss. She had an enormous, some might say morbidly obese, orange-tabby cat named Matisse. Matisse, fondly named after the infamous impressionist, Henri, was a cuddle buddy and he made a much better housemate than her ex, Jeffery, or *Ox* as everyone in college called him, ever was. The big townhouse in Queens, where Cozie and Ox lived, never felt like home. And Ox had never been the same after they moved in.

IN LIEU OF EATING

Their house had been in an up-and-coming neighborhood that was being revamped by wealthy yuppies. But to Cozie, it always felt sterile and out of place. And their presence in the neighborhood felt like a pretentious intrusion. When Cozie had asked to move closer to town, specifically her art classes and family, Ox went crazy. That time he'd only put his fist through the wall. But two days later, he'd become so enraged with Cozie, he put her in the hospital. After she was released, Cozie's dad and brothers retrieved her things from the big townhouse. She moved into her childhood bedroom, filed for divorce, and started trauma therapy.

She trudged more quickly now, eager to get to her home, *her* apartment. Cozie's apartment thrilled her. It was just a loft space. Her bed was also her couch. There was an easel where the kitchenette should be, but the natural light in the apartment persuaded her to forget all about a kitchen table and sit on the floor or kitchen counter to eat.

"*You aren't a dog? You're so disgusting. Why do you have to sit on the floor?*" Cozie shook her head, dismissing the villainous ghost that was mocking her. She whispered empowerment phrases. "*Shut up, Ox, you don't get to talk to me like that anymore.*"

She steadied the bags again, blinked wetness, not tears, from her eyes and pushed herself to her destination. Hot, dry, mechanical air pummeled her when she stumbled into the lobby of her apartment. It smelled like disinfectant and linoleum. Assuming 1945, linoleum had a smell.

Cozie saw the elevator doors begin to close, and a rush of adrenaline prompted her to run. Her slick boots slid as she ran on tiptoes, balancing her heavy grocery haul.

"*Wait*! Please hold the elevator!" She slipped toward the closing doors. The only rider, a tall but beefy man, ignored her pleas, but not before she leapt in, startling the doors with a clunk.

"*Thanks.*" Cozie breathlessly panted sarcastically. The man barely grunted. The doors closed, and Cozie attempted to push the elevator buttons with no free hands.

"Do you mind?" She snipped at the man. Again, he merely grunted. "Ten, please." The man, somewhat begrudgingly, punched the button, and the elevator began its ascent with a jerk and a whirling buzz. Cozie bit back a giggle as the man's eyes widened behind thick, black lashes. He reminded her of a tall, slimmer Sylvester Stallone.

"Relax." Cozie consoled him. "It's just old." He nodded. Cozie adjusted the bags on her hip again and blew at a wisp of long hair that had escaped a blue banana clip, perched haphazardly on the back of her head. "New in town?" She inquired.

Again, the man grunted, and Cozie checked the elevator buttons to see when this Neanderthal was getting off. Twelve, she noted the lit button and was relieved at least one of them would be vacating the elevator soon.

They stood in what Cozie considered awkward silence and what the stranger considered a melody as the elevator slowly clicked past 2, 3, 4. There was nowhere to look, which made the situation weirder. If Cozie looked straight ahead she was looking at their reflection in the mirrored doors. She opted to nuzzle her nose into the bags. Again the whirling sound squealed and moaned, followed by a hefty jerk. Then 5, 6, 7, and just past eight, just before Cozie was near her arrival, came the whirring sound, decibels higher than the last and much higher than Cozie had grown accustomed to. Then the light flickered, and the ravaged elevator jerked to an abrupt and violent stop, lunging Cozie forward and knocking both riders to their knees. An apple, two oranges, her fun cereal, and six cans of Ensure dietary supplement broke loose and rolled around on the linoleum floor. The fluorescent light flickered off, and a greenish backup light immediately sputtered to life. Neither of the riders spoke, they both stayed down, looking wild-eyed and shocked.

Finally, "What in the hell?" The man grabbed the railing and lifted himself to a stand. Cozie scurried on her hands and knees, picking up groceries. The man began violently punching buttons. Cozie snapped at him. "Don't make it worse!"

IN LIEU OF EATING

"I'm not making it worse!"

"Yes! You are!" She spat. "Just move!"

Cozie pulled herself up, dusting off her patchwork floral skirt while simultaneously pushing the tall man away. She opened an aged brass door below the panel of buttons, revealing a cream-colored rotary phone with no dial. She picked up and listened,

"Hello, Jim? It's Cozie, the elevator has stopped." She listened and then began again, this time louder, "Hello? Hello? Yes! Jim? It's me, Cozie, and..." She looked at the man, "Who are you?"

The man stared at her for a long time, visibly shaken by the calamity of being stuck in an elevator. "*Hellooo? Anybody home? Who are you?*" Cozie prodded.

"Jay." The man finally answered. "My name is Jay, Jay Black." Cozie raised a curious eyebrow, and without taking her huge gold eyes off him, she spoke into the receiver.

"Some guy named Jay Black, he was headed up to twelve, the elevator stopped." She listened and then said, "Well, okay, but hurry. I have ice cream." She replaced the receiver on the hook and turned to face Jay.

"*Jay Black?* That sounds mysteriously suspicious." Cozie said, bending to pick up cans of vanilla Ensure.

"It's just my name. And mysterious and suspicious are the same thing." Jay answered flatly, leaning against the wall. "What did the person on the phone say?"

"Actually, he said he didn't authorize you to be in the building." Cozie stared at the man. He had a dark olive complexion, silky and brown as if he'd just returned from a beach vacation. His dark hair was cut in a neat, crisp buzz, with a fuller mass of dark waves on top. He shuffled his feet, which were dressed in flat, black Doc Martin boots.

He shoved his hands into his worn blue jeans, and Cozie noticed bulging biceps through his gray hoodie. Before answering her, Jay pulled his black backpack off and squatted, digging through it.

96 MINUTES BETWEEN SEVEN AND EIGHT

"No." He hissed. "What did he say about getting us out of here?"

"He said he'd call the maintenance guy, he'll let us know in a few minutes. You didn't answer me." Cozie continued. "Jim, the doorman? He said he didn't let you in the building. What are you doing here?"

"I'm here to see Chuck Worley on twelve. The doorman wasn't at the desk when I came into the building." Jay failed to mention he'd opened a door in the alley, setting off an alarm to distract the doorman. Cozie fussed with the groceries, trying to arrange everything back where it had been. She couldn't remember seeing Jim as she hustled for the elevator, but she did know that there was a widower on twelve named Worley.

The phone buzzed, and Cozie answered. "Hello, Jim?" Her voice cracked with eager hope. *"An hour or more?"* Cozie yelped. "Jim, you have got to be kidding me?" She nodded and then begged, "Please see if you can get someone here sooner. Oh!" Cozie chirped, "Will you call Ms. Tuttle and tell her I am stuck in the elevator, but I picked up her prescriptions and protein shakes?" Cozie's shoulders relaxed, and she listened. "Yeah, okay. I know you'll do your best. What? Uh?" She eyed Jay up and down. "No, I'm fine. I don't think he's dangerous. Are you?" Cozie held the phone a few inches from her face. "Are you dangerous, *Jay Black?*"

She continued her stare at him, oblivious to how dangerous the next 96 minutes would prove to be, and the random threat two strangers stuck in an elevator could be to a future neither of them could contrive.

About the Author

Jami Amerine is an author and artist. She and her husband, Justin, of 30 years, live in Hawaii. Together they have six children, aged 8 to 27.

Jami is the author of Stolen Jesus: An Unconventional Search for the Real Savior, Scared Ground Sticky Floors: How Less Than Perfect Parents Can Raise (Kind of) Great Kids, Well Girl: An Inside Out Journey to Wellness, and Rest Girl: A Journey from Exhausted and Stressed to Entirely Blessed. Several fiction novellas and her first art devotional, 90 Days to Stress-Free: Renovating the House that Worry Built, is now available. Jami's art can be found in Home Goods and other national retailers and on her website.

Jami has a Master's of Education in Counseling Development from Hardin Simmons University and a Bachelor of Science in Family and Consumer Science from Abilene Christian University.

When not knocking out books in her office or painting daisies and roses in her studio, Jami and Justin are on Island adventures with their two young sons. They are advocates of foster care and adoption and enjoy cooking and doing anything outside. Connect with Jami on her website, jamiamerine.com.

Connect with Jami

Website: jamiamerine.com
Email: jami@jamiamerine.com

For publicity inquiries, please contact Jami's publicist,
Jeane Burgess at Jeane@talloak.media

For all business matters use "attn: Justin
as the subject to jami@jamiamerine.com

You can also email Justin to connect with
the following team members:

Literary Agent: Dave Schroeder
Art Agent: Blakely Bering

Made in the USA
Coppell, TX
26 August 2023

20811657R00120